Thank God she didn't leave him standing there like a fool.

She stepped forward and finally, finally, he had his wife in his arms, her hair flying behind her with each swing, her cheeks flushed and her eyes alive.

In the warm glow of lights strung overhead, her brown eyes glistened, her breath whispering across his skin as a twirl landed her close to his cheek. "I forgot you could dance like this."

"I believe I forgot, as well. But it feels good to see you smile."

"Keep dancing and I'll keep right on smiling, cowboy."

If only it could be that simple.

He felt the electricity hum in the rapidly diminishing space between them. Lips so close as they passed, heat and fire in their gaze. Need rose in his chest with each ragged breath.

A fat gray tabby pressed against his legs and hers, seeming to push them closer and closer. Until they were seconds, a mere breath away. And then she swayed into him, only a hint, but it was all the encouragement he needed to capture her lips.

* * *

TOP DOG DUDE RANCH

Dear Reader,

Welcome to Moonlight Ridge, Tennessee, home to the Top Dog Dude Ranch, renowned for family-friendly rustic retreats that heal broken hearts. Some say it's the majestic mountain vistas. Others vow there's magic in the hot springs. All agree, there's something special about the four-legged creatures at the Top Dog Dude Ranch that give guests a "new leash on love."

Thank you so much for picking up the first novel in my Top Dog Dude Ranch series, *Last-Chance Marriage Rescue*. I'm thrilled to say there are already more Top Dog adventures on the horizon! For more info on upcoming stories (and my own adventures with my canine buddies), check out my website, www.catherinemann.com.

Happy reading!

Cathy

Last-Chance Marriage Rescue

CATHERINE MANN

If you purchased this book without a cover you should be aware that this book is stolen property. It was reported as "unsold and destroyed" to the publisher, and neither the author nor the publisher has received any payment for this "stripped book."

Recycling programs for this product may not exist in your area.

ISBN-13: 978-1-335-40807-5

Last-Chance Marriage Rescue

Copyright © 2021 by Catherine Mann

All rights reserved. No part of this book may be used or reproduced in any manner whatsoever without written permission except in the case of brief quotations embodied in critical articles and reviews.

This is a work of fiction. Names, characters, places and incidents are either the product of the author's imagination or are used fictitiously. Any resemblance to actual persons, living or dead, businesses, companies, events or locales is entirely coincidental.

This edition published by arrangement with Harlequin Books S.A.

For questions and comments about the quality of this book, please contact us at CustomerService@Harlequin.com.

Harlequin Enterprises ULC
22 Adelaide St. West, 40th Floor
Toronto, Ontario M5H 4E3, Canada
www.Harlequin.com

Printed in U.S.A.

USA TODAY bestselling author **Catherine Mann** has won numerous awards for her novels, including both a prestigious RITA® Award and an *RT Book Reviews* Reviewers' Choice Award. After years of moving around the country bringing up four children, Catherine has settled in her home state of South Carolina, where she's active in animal rescue. For more information, visit her website, catherinemann.com.

Books by Catherine Mann

Harlequin Special Edition

Top Dog Dude Ranch

Last-Chance Marriage Rescue

Harlequin Desire

Alaskan Oil Barons

The Baby Claim
The Double Deal
The Love Child
The Twin Birthright
The Second Chance
The Rancher's Seduction
The Billionaire Renegade
The Secret Twin

Texas Cattleman's Club: Houston

Hot Holiday Rancher

Visit the Author Profile page
at Harlequin.com for more titles.

To Jim

Prologue

Kacie Archer swirled the lasso over her head, eyeing the blasted target.

Her twin sister, Kelsey.

Her *perfect* sister.

Except today Kelsey was being sneaky for once, using the computer in their dad's barn office when it was strictly off-limits. A total shocker since she never broke the rules. She'd always one-upped Kacie since the day she was born first. Kelsey even skipped ahead to the fifth grade this year, while Kacie was still struggling not to fall behind in the fourth. The only thing she did well? Rope and ride.

Things she wouldn't get to do anymore once they lost their family's dairy farm. Who knew when and where they would move?

This year might be her last chance to win the fall festival roping competition. And win in a higher age division.

Her version of skipping a grade.

She kicked through the bit of scattered straw on the pine floor and wondered how many more times she would get to hang out in her dad's barn office. She picked through memories of time spent in the office. Under the desk playing with Waffles when he was a kitten. Watching through a hole in the door as her dad delivered a calf. Wearing her uncle's favorite Stetson as a reward for doing her math homework. Uncle Tyler had always said he was cowboy at heart, not a dairy farmer.

Focus. Practice. Kacie finessed the rope snaking in lazy circles with just the right speed to keep it aloft, timing her motions in sync with the click, click, clicking of the milking machines beyond the office door. She took in the years of photos of the dairy farm covering the planked walls and willed away the urge to cry. Being angry at Kelsey was easier.

Kacie launched the lasso at Kelsey. The rippling loop soared like a dream in flight, just waiting to land, to grab hold and contain the target. Closer, closer, closer still it rippled.

And missed.

The rope smacked the old wood desk, startling the snoozing tabby cat into motion, which toppled a tin can full of pens. Waffles dodged markers and highlighters as they flew onto the computer keyboard.

Her twin shot to her feet, blue eyes flashing as pens rolled off onto the planked floor. "Hey, be careful. I've been working on this flyer for two hours." She grabbed the can and knelt in the middle of the mess. "I need to finish before Mom and Dad come back here."

"Why? Because you're scared you'll get in trouble for using the computer for some dumb school project without permission?" Kacie reeled in the rope.

"Of course I'm afraid of them finding out what I'm doing." She reached deep under the desk, her blond braids swinging forward. "You should be, too, since you've been sitting around watching me when you're still grounded for putting your backpack over that kid's head on the bus. Now finish cleaning up so I can get back to work."

"Do it yourself." Kacie adjusted the slipknot on her lasso, huffing a hank of hair off her sweaty forehead. "There's no way I'm helping you with anything after how you ratted me out."

"Not even if what I'm doing is to save our family?" She placed the can in its exact same spot on the desk, between a lamp and a paperweight made of horseshoes—a Father's Day gift Kelsey had made in art class.

"Last time I checked," Kacie said, "you weren't some magic genie able to give out miracles."

"Well, duh." Kelsey started typing again. "But I was looking around on the internet and found this place called the Top Dog Dude Ranch. It's in Moonlight Ridge, Tennessee. Doesn't that sound dreamy?"

Kacie grunted, using one foot to corral some highlighters into a pile.

Kelsey continued, "They do more than getaways for couples. They advertise family vacations. I think if we get them away from all the stress here, Mom and Dad will remember they love each other."

Fat chance of that.

"I thought you were the smart one. Those places cost a lot of money." She jammed the markers she'd gathered back into the can, then slithered her rope along the floor to lure Waffles from the windowsill.

"That's why I've been working on a fundraiser.

We're going to wash dogs. It'll be a secret, though. No spoiling the surprise." Kelsey turned the computer monitor toward Kacie, the screen filled with a picture of the two of them bathing their family dogs, their mom and dad smiling as they watched.

What a joke.

"I think that's a stupid idea." She knew it wasn't fair to snap at her sister. It wasn't Kelsey's fault she was so darn perfect. But there was so much sadness in their family these days, and a trip was only going to make it worse. "Don't you remember the last time we went on a vacation? They fought so hard over where to stop for lunch, we had to turn around before we even made it to the campground."

Anger chewed up her insides just thinking about that day. She'd been looking forward to exploring a cave like her parents promised. Just another broken promise because they got mad at each other.

"But the Top Dog Dude Ranch is special. Some say it's even magical with how they help families get better."

Frustration and sadness bubbled over. "That's bull. They're just trying to steal your money. You'd be better off saving up for a new tablet so you don't have to use Dad's computer or the school's Chromebook."

"Don't you want Mom and Dad to get back together?"

"I want them to stop fighting," she cried, then bit her lip. Hard.

She was tired of being sad all the time. Sad over her parents arguing about money. Sad because they were going to lose the farm since they were broke from taking care of Uncle Tyler after he got sick. Sad over Uncle Tyler dying.

Everything was changing.

Kelsey's shoulders sagged in defeat. "Fine. Keep playing with your rope. But just at least think about helping me."

"We would have to wash all the dogs in the entire state." Although that was the only halfway fun part about her sister's plan. Kacie loved dogs.

"I've done the math. It's cheaper since we would only have to drive two hours—which is also less time for Mom and Dad to fight in the car."

Her sister kinda had a point with that one. "I still think it's a scam."

"If you're right about the Top Dog Dude Ranch being a hoax, then they'll spend the whole week bickering and you can say 'I told you so.' Will that make you happy?"

"Maybe." Anything was better than how she felt now. At least people would quit pretending things might change for the better with her parents.

"Don't you want to prove you're right?" her sister taunted.

"How?"

"I'm glad you asked." Kelsey clicked more computer keys and the printer fired up, spitting out papers. "Help me raise the money and we can see which one of us is right."

Somehow she'd walked straight into the trap of helping her anyway. She sighed all the way to her feet, curling her rope back into a circle.

"Okay then." She clunked the lasso on the edge of the desk. "Even if we raise enough money to go, I'm not going to help you matchmake with some silly games that won't even work and will probably just make them fight with each other."

"You can do whatever you want once we get there. I've got the magic of Moonlight Ridge, Tennessee, on my side." She turned back to her seat. "If you keep throwing like you're doing today, you're gonna need some of that magic to win the competition."

Kacie dropped into a seat beside her sister and started folding flyers. "You're gonna eat those words when I win your stupid bet about this trip to the Top Dog Dude Ranch."

And in a flash she knew that going on this trip really was what she wanted most. What she wanted even more than winning that lasso competition. She wanted to stop waiting for the next explosion that would end everything. She was tired of never knowing when it would be time to move. So she was going to do everything possible to make this ill-fated family vacation happen.

After all the stress and tears over the last year, she wanted her parents to—finally—call it quits.

Chapter One

Four weeks later

"I'm ready to call it quits with Douglas." Nina Archer gripped her cell phone, wishing she could pour out her heart to her foster sister in person over a bottomless bowl of popcorn.

If ever she'd needed support in person, now was the time. Her eyes were still bleary from crying half the night.

Switching her cell onto speakerphone, Nina picked her way through the wooded trail behind the back pasture of her family's small dairy farm, praying the walk would ease her stress headache. "I just don't know what else to do, Ashlynn."

"Oh, no," her foster sister whispered, Ashlynn's voice cracking. "I really thought you two had what it takes. Do you want me to drive over?"

Yes.

Absolutely yes.

But she couldn't ask Ashlynn to spend the gas money. Her foster sister still lived in their small North Carolina hometown, working the same fast-food job she had when Nina left for college in Tennessee. When Nina felt tense about her own family's financial concerns, she reminded herself that Ashlynn struggled even harder. Yet she never failed to be a sounding board for her whenever Nina needed an ear.

"Thanks, but I'm okay." A lie. "I just need to vent."

Stepping over a rotted log, she shivered inside her long-sleeved thermal T-shirt. She'd hiked this path often in the past year—always alone—trying to exercise the frustration from her marriage. But no more. She had a line on a rental house and wanted to get settled before the holidays.

"Well, vent away. Take as long as you need. I'm alone on a Friday with just my laundry," Ashlynn said, the sounds of a Laundromat echoing in the background. “What did you two fight about this time?”

Ashlynn always had been able to read her. The day Nina’s caseworker took her to her fourth foster home—Nina’s world shattered by her parents’ death in a boating accident—Ashlynn had been sitting on the front steps eating a bag of supersalty french fries. She’d invited Nina to sit and share the fries, one of the few perks of working in fast food. Their bond had been forged that day, cemented by their need to connect. Ashlynn had come from a volatile household and craved peace and routine. Nina had been grieving for her parents and had been naturally quiet, so Ashlynn had liked to be near her.

Although there had been nothing quiet about her and Douglas’s life lately. She’d been in constant turmoil for years.

“It’s gotten so bad, we barely even argue anymore. We don’t even talk about the most basic things. The silence is worse than the fights. I know we’ve had our challenges.” They’d married so young and so fast, since she’d been pregnant. There were times she felt like they’d never had a meaningful conversation. “But I really thought once the twins survived those first terrifying weeks in neonatal ICU, the rest would be smooth sailing. We had no idea the heartache waiting just around the corner with Douglas's brother and then financial struggles."

"You've both been under a lot of stress, especially lately."

Of course, Ashlynn knew that all too well since they talked often. And Nina had needed her foster sister more than ever once Douglas closed down even more. His brother's death had hit him hard. They'd all grieved for Tyler.

How could such a simple fall from a ladder while fixing a roof go so horribly wrong? When they found Tyler passed out, they thought he'd just suffered from a concussion, then learned it was an aneurysm that caused him to lose his balance. By the time doctors made the diagnosis, there'd been so much irreversible damage, he'd spent the final seven years of his life needing constant care, mentally so very present but physically wasting away.

And now, with bankruptcy looming?

It was too much.

"I just wish the stress could have brought us together rather than driven us apart." She paused as a fox scampered past. How naive to have ever thought their marriage was bulletproof. "About six months ago, he said he wanted to get a vasectomy."

That had spurred a fight they still hadn't recovered from and resulted in them moving into separate bedrooms.

"Do you want more kids? I thought you want to leave."

"I don't know if I want more children. Heaven knows we're barely making ends meet, which is why we kept delaying having another baby." He'd argued that the need to stop having kids was about more than the day-to-day expenses of a child. What if she got pregnant and she had to go on bed rest again? Or if they had another premature delivery, how would they afford the NICU bills? She didn't have answers. "I just know I'm not ready to close that door."

"Was that what today's fight was about?"

"No, it was about money. Again. He wants to just give up and sell the farm. He won't even discuss why. I told him about a job opening for a teacher's aide in a neighboring county and he was adamantly against it." His pride had been stung, not that he said a word. "I'm just so tired of trying to save a marriage that's in name only."

"How are the girls taking the news?"

Her heart broke all over again just thinking about how to tell them. For once, they were actually getting along, thanks to their dog-washing business. She didn't even care that they wouldn't tell her what they planned to buy with their income.

"The girls don't know yet, Ashlynn." Grief stole

her breath and she rested a palm against the trunk of a maple tree, leaves a vibrant canopy of autumn colors. “I’m trying to figure out how we should tell them. The timing is just so awful. They haven’t had a chance to finish grieving for their uncle.”

So much sadness, so much loss, so many dreams shattering. Looking back, she could see she’d been in search of a family and thought Douglas could provide just that. With his sprawling dairy farm and shoulders big enough to carry the burdens of the world, he would never let anyone down.

But all too soon, she’d become pregnant with twins, a high-risk pregnancy. She’d left college, ending her studies to become a professional photographer. Still, Douglas had reassured her, telling her not to worry. Once the babies were born, he and his brother would split the work on the farm. They would pull double duty with the babies, and she could return to school. And they had helped. And helped.

There had certainly been plenty to do, leaving them all exhausted. As she’d fallen into bed each night in Douglas’s arms, she’d reminded herself there was plenty of time to finish her studies.

Then life happened with Tyler’s accident…

The crisp air of autumn crept in to cool the evening air. Twigs crunched under her feet. There were countless opportunities for photos, from a fall warbler to a flash of turkey tail feathers. But her creative spirit was pure gray today, the pain so deep she couldn't even channel her grief into art.

Ashlynn continued, "At least promise me you'll come here if you need me. My roommate moved out, so I have the space. Even if you just want to get away for a while."

"Thank you. I'll keep it in mind." She missed having someone to talk to, the isolation of the farm wrapping around her all the more since his brother died and they eventually had to let their last worker go. "If I do take you up on the offer, I promise the girls and I won't stay with you for long. I just need time to finish locking down plans."

She intended to take the job as a teacher's aide, even though Douglas had objected. The marriage was over anyway, and she would need to support herself and the girls. There wouldn't be any assets to divide since the dairy farm was struggling.

"You're welcome to stay however long you need. I owe you for the six months you and Douglas let me camp out in the barn's studio apartment when I lost my place."

"You helped us on the farm." Since Douglas's brother had moved out of the bachelor pad into the main farmhouse after his accident, it had only made sense to offer the space to Ashlynn. In return, she helped on the farm to pick up the slack while Tyler recovered.

Except he never did regain his health. He'd needed full-time care.

They'd spent all their extra money and energy trying to keep him comfortable. After all, he'd given up his baseball scholarship to bring up Douglas after their parents' death.

The brothers had been so very close. Not like her daughters. Would some time at Ashlynn's help them? "I wouldn't want you to feel obligated."

"We're sisters. It's what we do."

Foster siblings, but closer in some ways than bios because of their shared losses.

"Thanks, Ashlynn," for then, for now, "and I love you. I'll be in touch soon."

Disconnecting the call, but not their connection, she tucked the cell into the front pocket of her hoodie and started back up the path toward the homestead, her headache still in full swing as she tried to decide what to do next.

At least the girls weren't engaged in open warfare for once, thanks to the dog washing. She hated to upend their world. She knew all too well how deeply loss at a young age could mark a person. She hated bringing even an ounce of pain to her daughters' lives.

As if divorce weren't bad enough. They would

likely lose their home, too, once the bank stepped in. The farm had been struggling for a while, and when Covid first gripped the world forcing businesses to close, there'd been nowhere to sell their milk. Schools had continued to supply milk for free lunches, but that contract hadn't been enough to pull their business out of a deep financial ditch.

What kind of future would she be able to offer her children?

The sound of dogs barking in the distance made her think of her girls having to say goodbye to the farm animals. No rental home in her limited price range would accommodate their menagerie. She could already imagine the tears when the girls would have to say goodbye to their pet chicken, Pixie, that her husband couldn't bring himself to turn into dinner when the bird had stopped producing eggs a year ago.

She pressed a hand to her temple, her headache growing, the noise from the barking dogs sparking pain behind her eyes. Except they didn't sound like any of her dogs. Tree branches rustled behind her, giving her only an instant's warning to turn.

Just as a pack of shaggy wet canines plowed straight at her.

Douglas had a real love-hate relationship with this particular tractor.

He stalked away from the field in disgust, leaving the rotary tiller in the middle of the field. Old Bessie had given them a lot of years, and no amount of new parts would resurrect her.

Kind of like his marriage.

The land that usually comforted him currently had his heart in his throat. This day had been a train wreck from the start. He hadn't been able to concentrate, not with thoughts of Nina walking away with tears in her eyes. He just couldn't face failing her anymore.

Their icy standoff sent her out on a walk to take solace from behind the lens of her camera. He could still see the tears in her eyes when he'd ignored all her hints to talk. Even thinking about those tears had him so distracted he almost bumped into the rope ladder dangling from the old tree house his brother had made for him in an ancient oak.

He would have to sell his farm soon, land that had belonged to Archers for over a hundred and fifty years. He'd done his best to take care of his brother and keep the farm intact. He hadn't imagined it would cost him his marriage. His family.

A scream split the air and he was more than grateful for any distraction from all the ways he'd failed every member of his family.

Adjusting the bill on his battered ball cap, he

tucked his head and darted past the fort, mildewed with age. So many accidents could happen on a farm. He knew that all too well. If Nina had been hurt…

He sprinted across the field, leaving behind the broken tractor he'd been trying to resurrect. Right now, every instinct was focused on finding his wife. Her shout had come from the opposite direction of the house. He'd lived on this land his whole life. He knew every inch, each divot in the dirt, every tree and root.

How much farther? Was that a child's squeal riding the wind? He charged into the clearing, prepared to defend his family from this threat, at least.

Then stopped short.

Nina was tangled in a pile of soggy pooches along with Kacie and Kelsey. Screams and squeals took shape into giggles and laughter. His daughters shot to their feet and chased a galloping yellow Labrador. His beautiful wife was being "trampled" by a poodle mix while a nimble collie leaped back and forth over her long, jean-clad legs. Nina's wavy blond hair shielded her face, then she swept the silky length back to reveal her face. His breath caught just as it had the first time he'd seen her. It was like she brought sunshine to his dark world.

His heart hammering in his ears, he took in her

smile scrunching her uptipped nose. Her sparkling golden-brown eyes.

Her wet flannel shirt.

He dragged his eyes off her alluring curves and back onto the chaos. The laughter. Such a rare occurrence these days he'd almost forgotten what it sounded like, what it felt like, to have his girls happy. All three of his girls—his wife and his daughters.

And this moment was too emotional, by far. He walled off his feelings and strode closer, boots crunching dried leaves.

"What's going on?" He shot out a hand to snag the Lab by the collar. "Is everyone all right?"

The dog shook a spray of water right in Douglas's face.

Kelsey giggled. "Be still, Digger."

Kacie hooked a leash around the collie's neck. "We were washing dogs. This is Lucy, and Mom's got Peaches."

He shot a glance back at Nina. She shrugged, avoiding his gaze as she tucked the poodle—Peaches—against her chest. Kneeling, Douglas braced a hand on her back as she stood. The heat of her seared through the damp cotton and into his senses.

"Girls," he said, "this fundraiser of yours isn't worth much if you lose a dog."

Or get hurt.

Nina cleared her throat self-consciously. "Maybe we could help. I don't want to discourage them from being charitable."

"And I don't want them racing around the farm on their own chasing other people's pets. It's become a safety issue. I'm putting a stop to this."

"No," Kelsey shouted, her braids dripping with water. "You can't."

Kacie pulled another leash out of her backpack and passed it to her sister. "I told you this wasn't going to work."

Nina's brown eyes narrowed. "What wasn't going to work? Kelsey?" She turned to the other twin. "Kacie?"

"Fine," Kacie sighed. "We weren't saving for charity. Well, not the way you mean. And we need to finish washing these guys because we've already been paid, and we owe a lot of money."

"You owe money?" His pride stung as he wondered what it was that his children needed that he'd been unable to provide.

Clutching the poodle, Nina faced down her daughters. "Do you mean you've been lying to us, letting us think you were raising money for charity?"

Kacie's chin jutted. "We need charity. We're poor."

And the hits to his ego just kept coming.

Nina tucked a blond strand of hair behind Kacie's ear. "We're not poor. We have the farm."

Not for long, though. Douglas had to know. "If you weren't raising money for charity, what were you saving up for that we haven't been able to give you?"

Kelsey tugged at her braid the way she always did when she was lying…or thinking up a lie.

Kacie elbowed her sister. "Go ahead and tell them. It was your bright idea."

Nina stepped alongside Douglas for the first time in longer than he could remember. It stunned him still for an instant, and apparently, he wasn't the only one. The girls were staring at them with identical blue eyes so wide he almost laughed. Almost. Humor was nowhere in sight for him these days.

A wide grin spread across Kelsey's face. "We were saving up to buy a vacation at the Top Dog Dude Ranch."

"The Top Dog what?" Nina asked, shifting the poodle in her arms, which brushed her elbow against his.

He forced his focus onto his daughters and not leaning closer to his wife.

"It's a place for family vacations. You know my friend Simone?" Kelsey asked, then rushed ahead before anyone could answer. "Well, her mom booked a trip after she got remarried. The vacation was to help everyone get along better and it worked."

Her words sucker punched Douglas, and judging by Nina's soft gasp, she'd been caught equally off guard by the pain in their daughter's voice. Although now that he thought about it, he remembered Simone's stepdad giving a glowing account of the Top Dog Dude Ranch and what a great place it was to decompress. While he couldn't dodge the sense of foreboding that the girls were matchmaking, didn't he need all the help he could get if he wanted to save his marriage?

Kacie eyed them with a cynicism far too dark for a child her age. "It's been forever since we had a family vacation. Sounds fun, doesn't it?"

Chapter Two

Fun?

A *fun* vacation?

Being trapped with her soon-to-be ex, with her heart breaking and their children always watching with those wide, hopeful eyes as they waited for an outcome that could never happen? That sounded more like a nightmare. One that she desperately and feverishly tried to wake from. No dice. Every movement led back to her stomach-plummeting sadness. Especially when she took in the spark of hope glistening from the twins.

Not that fun like that was even possible. There was no way they could afford to hire the help needed to care for the farm in their absence. Vacations had been an unattainable dream for a very long time.

Nina glanced at Douglas, trying to gauge his reaction, and yes, hoping he might have a solution that would pacify the twins. But nope. His lips had gone tight in that way they did when his pride was hurt. Or his heart. Except she knew his emotions weren't in a turmoil over her. He always had a weak spot when it came to the girls. That was one of the reasons she'd held on for so long. He loved their daughters, and they worshipped him.

Kacie leaned down to brush twigs out of Lucy's shaggy coat, but kept her wide eyes trained on her parents. Birch bark rained onto the yellowing grass. "Dad, please, please, we really want to go. They have so many fun things to do."

"But Champ…" Douglas swept off his ball cap and dropped it on top of her head. "You already live on a farm."

"It's not the same." Her chapped little hands adjusted the bill.

Kelsey secured her hold on the Labrador as the pup's tongue slid lazily out of the side of its mouth. "This one's magical. I read all about it."

Douglas studied her with a suspicious glint in his blue eyes. "Kelsey, where did you read that?"

That sure made this sound like more than a whim.

Her shoulders braced. “I went to the place’s website. I did my research.”

Images filled her mind of her little scholar hunched over a desk with notebooks, pens and highlighters. Her nose scrunched as she pored over a list of pros and cons for different places. Always so judicial, so focused. So committed to a vision of how she thought things should be. Kelsey had taken it especially hard that there wasn’t any science or research that could save Uncle Tyler. Just as Kacie had struggled with understanding that it didn’t matter how hard she worked to bring her uncle blankets and snacks, fluffing his pillow and asking for advice on lassoing, he didn’t recover.

“Research?” Kacie snorted. “Of course you did loads and loads of research, just like the way you laze around reading while I do your chores.”

Kelsey pivoted fast, her soggy sneakers digging into the mud. “You don’t have to be rude.”

“I just mean that the magic thing isn’t going to convince them of anything.” Kacie shifted her attention back to her father. “It’s a vacation ranch. Not a working ranch. We could do all the things we really like about living on the land and none of the bothersome or messy stuff.”

“Yeah,” Kelsey said, “like mucking out stalls.”

Kacie nodded. “Or getting up at five in the morning.”

"Or cleaning the chicken coop," Kelsey added.

"Or getting up at five in the morning," Kacie repeated.

"Or getting pitched off a pony."

Kacie grinned, glancing over at the barn. "Not all of us have that particular problem."

"That's not the point," Kelsey sighed, the wind rustling the branches overhead. "We just really want a nice vacation. As a family."

Leaning against each other, the girls leveled a commanding stare at their parents.

Nina's chin quivered, too sad for words. Douglas's wince hurt her bruised heart even more. He already worried about the children not getting to be kids. On that much, they agreed. Nina stressed about that, too.

Nina dusted dried fall leaves off her daughter's hair. "Maybe another time."

Pieces of orange and brown leaves from a black gum tree disintegrated between her fingertips, giving her mind an anchor for the waves of emotion that pushed against her rib cage and threatened her smile.

"Girls—" Douglas shifted from boot to boot "—perhaps you could go with your mom."

Surprise rippled through her that he would even make the suggestion. She wanted to think it was because he really needed to care for the animals.

But a part of her heart whispered that he would be glad to have her gone. The reality of her marriage disintegrating as tangibly as the dried-out fall leaves hit home, whispering inside her. This was real, real, real.

Both girls went stock-still. Kelsey's lip quivered. Kacie's shoulders slumped.

Douglas scrubbed a hand over his square jaw. "I need to stay here and work the farm."

"But, Dad," Kelsey pleaded, "it won't be the same without you."

Kacie pulled off the ball cap and passed it back to her father. "We'll work harder to help you get ready. Right, Kelsey?"

She elbowed her twin, though her eyes stayed trained on her dad with a roper's focus. Assessing the target. Calculating the next move.

Kelsey clapped her chest. "I'll clean the chicken coop *and* the stalls."

Douglas scrubbed a hand through his hair before dropping the hat back in place. "Your mom and I will talk about it."

Both girls turned their hopeful eyes to her.

Nina felt like a pinned butterfly, wanting to escape but knowing it was in her children's best interest to have this discussion. "Yes, we will discuss it."

Douglas took the poodle from Nina, his hand

brushing her waist. Her breath caught in her rib cage, her heart fluttering like that trapped butterfly. Her gaze met his and held; he froze for a charged instant.

Then he blinked, breaking the connection, and passed the poodle to Kacie. "Now take the dogs and scram."

The girls' laughter carried on the breeze long after they and the dogs faded from view, swallowed by a shower of autumn leaves drifting from the hawthorn and yellow bud trees.

Douglas hadn't felt this low-down since he'd had to deplete the bank account to buy meds for his brother, only to learn his daughters needed school shoes. He'd sold off a rodeo championship belt buckle. How could Nina have ever even entertained the idea of more kids when they could barely afford the ones they had? And why did she keep insisting he pour good money after bad to save the farm? If he sold now, at least they could avoid bankruptcy.

He felt like such a failure, he couldn't stop himself from retreating from his wife. He knew he couldn't give her what she wanted. Avoiding her was easier than arguing about money and all the ways he fell short in pouring his feelings out on command.

Hitching his hands on his hips, he breathed in a steadying breath and tried to ignore the apple scent of his wife's shampoo. He knew the vacation request was just a cover for something they wanted more, something else he hadn't been able to give them. A family repaired, unified.

But they'd gone past that point. Years of hard work and loss had worn them down until they were worse than angry. They'd both gone numb.

Boots pressed into the slick soil, leaving craters in his wake. Pretty much like his life. Holes everywhere.

His kids deserved to have their family stay intact. Even if he and Nina had somehow lost their way to loving each other under the weight of bills and work, he still wanted to keep them all under one roof, for the sake of their daughters.

"That sure was a sucker punch." He hated thinking of the girls longing for the perfect family vacation. He wasn't so sure he could make that happen at even some supposedly magic ranch.

Nina sagged back against the roughened trunk of a pecan tree, her forehead furrowed, her mouth thinning with tension. "I can't believe they've been planning this all along with the dog washing, making us believe it was for charity."

"Or that they think we are some kind of charity." A point that stung more than a little.

"Well," she said, hugging her arms over her damp top and shivering, "they aren't wrong that we're in trouble."

He shrugged out of his jean jacket for his wife, remembering too well the days when he would have draped it over her shoulders and tucked her against his side. Now there was nothing more than a phantom warmth for what felt like a lifetime ago. Those days were past. "We've been careful to shield them from the worst."

During the virus scare, so many contracts defaulted. Restaurants closed. Conferences were canceled along with their big power meals full of heavy creams and cheeses. Forget about farmers' markets.

But he'd tried to be a good man in hard times. Rather than dumping their milk, they'd given away farm goods to other families in need. Still, none of it helped him numb the blow to his pride over how much he was failing his wife and kids.

Notes of a lone songbird cut through the forest. A sad, subdued call that echoed through the trees. His life had fallen apart and he had no idea how to make it right.

Nina touched his arm lightly. "Just because we haven't told them doesn't mean they haven't sensed it." She took the jacket from him warily and hugged it to her chest. “We live under the same roof.”

“Not for much longer,” he said softly. “That’s what you’re thinking, right?”

Her honey-brown eyes went so very sad. “We both know it’s inevitable.”

“Do we?” He couldn’t stop himself from asking, from hoping there was some way to salvage his family. Even if he and Nina had lost the love they’d once shared, at least he wouldn’t lose his kids.

She lifted a hand in protest. “Oh, Douglas, you know there’s nothing left for us to try.”

Pain lanced through him. He knew it, and yet couldn’t possibly bring himself to admit it out loud, because what kind of life would he have without her?

One deep breath in of Archer land sent him back to another time on this path, the day he met Nina during her photography project. She’d laughed freely with him, the spark between them so strong and new.

An idea formed in his mind, taking root with each breath. “Then prove it.”

“What do you mean?” She straightened from the tree, her blond ponytail sliding and calling to his fingers.

“Let’s give the girls what they want.” The more

he said, the more certain he become that this was the right approach. "Let's tell them we'll go to the Top Dog Dude Ranch."

Her jaw went slack with shock. "You can't be serious."

"I am. Completely."

She shrugged into the jacket, avoiding his eyes, jaw tight. Then she exhaled one of those resigned sighs he'd heard more often than not of late. "Even if I agreed, a place like that must have a waiting list a mile long."

Probably. But that wouldn't stop him from trying to buy more time to salvage the mess he'd made of his marriage. "Then at least the twins will hear that we didn't tell them no. That's one less disappointment for us to heap on them."

"What if the place actually does have an opening and we can somehow afford it?" Her voice grew with exasperation. "Do you intend for us to go through with the trip? Even if that means we have to pretend we're a big happy family?"

"If there's an opening and we can somehow pay for it—" Even saying those words chewed at his pride. "If all lines up, we can give them the vacation they want. And when we tell them their parents might be splitting—"

"Are splitting," she interjected.

He stifled the urge to just walk away. It was

hard to be around each other when she was so quick to remind him he wasn't worth sticking around for.

"Fine," he conceded, reaching over her to grip a branch, catching a handful of yellowing leaves. "To tell them that their parents are splitting. They will have seen that we can still be civil to each other."

"And you believe we can be civil to each other?" she pressed him, fine brows arching. Skeptical. Wary.

He hated that they'd come to this.

Sighing, he gave the only answer he could. "I hope that we can. If we can't, we have to figure out how."

He just prayed those words wouldn't be needed. Although he also knew it would take every bit of magic the Top Dog Dude Ranch had to offer for him to figure out a way to repair his marriage.

But he'd already lost all the family he'd had: his parents and then brother. Nina had lost hers as well.

He refused to let either of them suffer one more loss.

Nina sat on the edge of the stone hearth, the only spot available with the great room so full of suitcases and duffels. She jabbed the needle through the tear in Kacie's sleeping bag. Shock still had her nearly speechless, leaving her almost a zombie going through the motions of packing.

This space had always been the hub of the family, so much so, she'd struggled with how to put her stamp on the space. Then they'd moved the table from the big picture window to put a hospital bed for Tyler at the end, to keep him a part of the family moments. The bed was gone, but they still hadn't brought the table back.

She shook off depressing memories and focused on the present.

By some crazy miracle, they would be at the Top Dog Dude Ranch only seven days after learning of the girls' request. A mixed blessing. The girls had gotten their wish to have the family together, but at what cost?

Right after telling the twins they would try to go, Nina had contacted the ranch. Not only had there been a last-minute cancellation, but the family that canceled had also requested their prepayment be applied to another family. Their entire trip was free. She would have sworn it was a setup, orchestrated by the girls, but the lady taking reservations genuinely did not seem to know who they were.

It was surreal. A coincidence beyond believing. So either it had to be a setup, or the biggest piece of luck she'd ever experienced. That made her insides skitter with nerves. Wary of when the rug would be pulled from under her, when this little bit of happiness for her family would crumble, too.

Douglas had been as shocked as she was. He didn't reveal much about his feelings, but she'd been able to see the surprise in his eyes. And the relief. It was so sad to think how long it had been since news of any kind had made her husband appear anything less than weighted down by worries. Not that it changed anything between them, but she still empathized with how hard life had been for him, too.

Once the girls let news about the trip leak to their dog-washing clientele, neighbors had reached out with offers to watch their place for free. They'd insisted that it was the least they could do after all the free milk and beef when the town had been struggling.

Her eyes watered even now at their generosity, especially after she'd felt so alone out here for so long. Those tears threatened to well over altogether at the notion of leaving those friends and neighbors behind when she took the teaching job in the next county. While they would still be close in miles, she and the girls would be very far away from their dreams.

She shifted on the stone hearth and took in the

sight of her daughters across the family room. Kelsey sat cross-legged on the floor with an inventory list and a pencil. Kacie was all motion, digging through the suitcases, backpacks and canvas bags, shouting out items to check off. Clothes, gear, snacks for the road. An unbelievable amount of luggage, as if packing wasn't already awkward enough when she and her husband wouldn't even be sharing a bed. The irony wasn't lost on her that there was no need for a vasectomy when they weren't even having sex.

Kelsey sorted granola bars into four lunch boxes. Measured. Methodical. "I can't believe we really get to go the dude ranch."

Nina inspected the stitched hole in the sleeping bag and found it tightly sealed. "It's what you wanted, what you worked for. And yes, it's really happening." She looped the thread into a knot, then snipped it off. "Well, it will if we can ever finish packing."

Kelsey read items off the list, chewed yellow pencil in hand. "Boots. Gloves. Hat."

"Check," Kacie confirmed. "I packed those first off."

"And I packed extra wool socks. It's colder there than here."

"Great. Do you think you could have picked somewhere warmer when you researched?"

Kelsey set down the list on the old hickory coffee table, yellow pencil rolling. "There's fly-fishing and archery."

"Huh," Kacie mumbled, stringing an imaginary bow. "Are you the target?"

"Girls, that's enough." She should have known their truce would be short-lived.

Nina hated seeing them fight like this. They'd had little tiffs in the past, but nothing like their tussles of the past few months. She couldn't help but wonder if the blame lay in how much she and Douglas argued, all the tension that came in the aftermath. If so, why would the twins want to spend even more time together?

Suspicion teased at her. "Why did you decide to push for this trip, to this particular place?"

The twins fell mute, glancing from one to the other with that air of the unspoken language of twins. Utterly unified in this moment by a bond that defied any dispute.

Finally, Kacie took a step forward. "Like we said. We wanted a family trip since it's been such a long time."

Kelsey concurred with a tight nod.

"Still, girls, there are other dude ranches around that are a lot less expensive." She raised a hand quickly. "Not that I'm complaining about the price, since everything worked out better than we could have hoped. I'm just curious what made you pick this particular place. Come on, the more we know the more we can help you with whatever you're planning."

Kelsey pushed aside the bags and climbed over a vintage suitcase to sit at Nina's feet. "They have other classes, too."

Kacie interrupted, "They call them pack-tivities. Get it? A group of dogs is a pack? Pack-tivities."

Kelsey continued, "There are even pack-tivities that are indoors, that help people get along better. We think that would be good, uh, for me and for Kacie. Maybe you and Dad could join us."

A sigh of resignation pushed through her. She'd suspected something was up, but this was so much more heart-tugging than she could have guessed. What child asked for something that amounted to therapy? Not many. Which told her just how hurt and desperate they were.

She looked at the vintage suitcase, a relic from her days in foster care. Life had stretched before her with that old green suitcase in hand, finally in control of her own life. Possibilities as numerous as blades of grass. She'd had such hopes for building a family of her own someday, only to let her girls down.

While the outcome wasn't going to be what they

hoped, they truly could use all the healing help the Top Dog Dude Ranch had to offer.

She held out her hand. "Pass me the printouts. I want to start marking which events we'll be attending."

Chapter Three

Douglas draped his wrist over the steering wheel, his truck eating up the miles in the two-hour drive east from his farm to the Top Dog Dude Ranch. The fall palette outside was a blur of oranges, yellows and reds he hadn't taken the time to appreciate in longer than he could remember. His head was still spinning over how fast this trip had come together.

Seven days ago, he would have never guessed he would get a second chance to keep his family. Mountains dipped and rose as he guided the truck along the winding road. Steady hands for what he hoped was an equally steady future. He didn't intend to blow the opportunity.

Glancing in the rearview mirror, he checked on the twins, who were unusually quiet. Kelsey held her school-issued Chromebook, plowing through homework the teacher had sent with them. Kacie even had her Chromebook out as well, except one quick glance showed she was studying roping techniques rather than arithmetic. But at least they were quiet and happy, earbuds in place and unable to overhear anything he had to say to Nina.

He shot a look at his wife sitting across the bench seat in his old Ford. She rested her forehead against the passenger-side window, looking even more beautiful than the first day he saw her. She still stole the air from his lungs.

Back when they'd first met, she would have seized every moment of the journey with her camera, her gaze and lens capturing the most humbling, beautiful moments tucked away into landscapes and crevices of everyday life.

Now, she just looked…

Lost.

He scratched a hand over the ache in his chest and searched for something to say. He tucked his tongue against his cheek until he settled on something safe, easy. "What all did you and the girls bring?"

The truck was jam-packed full of luggage.

She jolted before looking back at him, then glanced over her shoulder, blond hair sliding over her cheekbones. “Kelsey swore it was all on the list.”

“I think we may be overprepared.” He checked the rearview mirror as a low-slung red sports car accelerated, then whipped past on the narrow country road.

A smile almost tugged her lips upward. Almost. “I think you could be right.”

He sent a grin her way, enjoying the shared levity for once rather than their usual arguments—or worse, silent tension. His grip tightened on the steering wheel as he guided the pickup on a hairpin turn, a wall of rocks dotting the mountainside. “Thank you for agreeing to come along. It means a lot to me to be able to offer this to the girls.”

Shadows whispered through her eyes like dark clouds muting the sky. “You have to know I’ll be sure you have time with them.”

Custodial visitation? He definitely didn’t want to talk about that. Sidestepping the version of his life where his family fractured, he nudged the conversation. “I’m still blown away by how the town rolled out to help watch over the farm so we could come here. They all have their own lives and businesses to look after.”

"They seemed glad to have a way to show their gratitude for the milk and beef during the pandemic." Her hands splayed on her knees, scratching along denim as she did when trying to hold her emotions in check.

"That was your idea." He didn't know why he'd been surprised when she suggested it. She loved the people of their small town. He'd just kicked himself for not thinking of it himself. "I don't deserve any credit."

"You would have come to the same conclusion," she dismissed. "I just thought of it a second before you."

He didn't intend to waste this time together arguing. "I feel like we haven't had a chance to catch our breath since then. These couple of weeks away could be a good thing."

"Good in what way?" The question came out as more of a plea. She hugged her lined jean jacket tighter around her. "Other than giving the girls a happy memory before we pull out the rug from under them."

"Are you regretting the decision to take the trip?" He turned the heater vents in her direction. Streams of warm air lifted her hair around her face.

"Not regretting it so much as just worried about how they'll handle what's coming afterward." She checked the rearview mirror that showcased the twins still glued to their screen time. Nina looked back at him. "Did we just use this trip as an excuse to delay telling the girls about our split?"

Uh, yeah, he had. But he wasn't admitting that to her. "The twins asked for this and by some miracle it's actually happening. Let's not question that. Can we agree to be in the moment and just enjoy our time at the ranch?"

A long sigh shuddered through her. "I'm sure determined to try."

If only he could hold her to that—to enjoying the moment and not worrying about what the future held—that opened a whole world of possibilities for him. When was the last time he'd romanced his wife? He needed to dust off his skills if he wanted any shot at keeping his family together. When they'd been dating, she loved nature hikes, ending with romantic picnics. Her favorite had been wine with fresh goat cheese from his farm.

So simple. And yet somehow, he'd let even the simple joys in life slip away. How had they gone from being a happy family to such a hot mess? "I, uh, saw on the brochure that they have quite a few hiking options."

She glanced at him in surprise. "That would be nice. The place is called Moonlight Ridge, after all."

A moonlight walk? That was promising. “What are some things you’d like to do? You should make the most of the vacation.”

“Well, there’s an ice cream parlor the girls would—”

“You. I said what would *you* like to do?”

Her brows pinched together. “I’m not sure. I’ll have to look at the list again.”

“There’s a couples’ massage.” He couldn’t resist taunting her with a wink.

She arched an eyebrow. “Don’t push your luck.”

He chuckled, the sound feeling alien in his throat. His artistic wife had often accused him of being too practical, too unemotional. He hadn’t seen his analytical nature as a detriment. In fact, he’d considered it an asset that kept the dairy farm afloat long after others in the industry folded.

But right now, he certainly wouldn’t mind a bit more emotional insight as to what made his wife tick. And if that meant attending every “workshop” Nina chose at the Top Dog Dude Ranch, then so be it.

As he focused on the future, the landscape collapsed around him in a wash of yellows and orange. Wind tunneled through the mountains, so strong, even the truck rocked. His thoughts plowed ahead to the Top Dog Dude Ranch and whatever waited for them there. Not that he believed in the magic his daughters rambled on about. But he did believe in hard work. In the ability to put in the time to change his fate, his family's course.

A flash out of the corner of his eye yanked his attention back on the road just as a white-tailed deer bolted into their path. He steered hard to avoid the buck, reflexes quick from growing up in the backwoods. A deer could take out a car—and everyone in it.

He definitely needed to rein in his emotions and set his mind to putting his life back in order.

Thank goodness they'd arrived at the Top Dog Dude Ranch without encountering any other deer leaping across the road. Surely that's what had her heart hammering against her rib cage. Not the prospect of sharing a romantic cabin with her husband for the next two weeks.

The playful conversation with Douglas had stirred hope she couldn't afford to feel. And a couples' massage?

She refused to let her thoughts go there for even an instant.

The girls radiated excitement from the back seat until the air all but hummed with it. Kacie and Kelsey had rolled down their windows and were leaning into the breeze despite the chill, sunlight dappling their faces. They pointed out and read signs that were posted giving directions, wooden and painted paw prints leading the way.

She opened her window, too, and drew in bracing breaths of fresh mountain air to steady her nerves. Phone still gripped in her hand from checking in, she chewed her lips as Douglas navigated up the winding mountain path. Towering pines grew around deep-set ancient boulders, the trees scenting the air with a hint of Christmas.

All these years later, Tennessee still made her breath catch. Spoke to the youngest parts of her soul. A part of her that, in spite of all the hardships, still yearned for the rush of mountain air, the gentle smallness of being out here.

And then the road narrowed while the trees parted to reveal a retreat so perfect it could have been straight from long-ago dreams shared while sitting on the porch with her foster sister. No doubt, the mountains had always called to her.

But this place?

It sparked with life. Fallen leaves sprinted along the yellowing grass like a gentle hearth fire from some fairy tale she couldn't quite remember.

The main lodge they'd passed moments ago felt stately. Sprawling like a rustic castle nestled in the foothills of towering mountains.

Douglas was all eyes forward, hands roving on the steering wheel as he kept the truck on the narrow road. For a moment, her heart surged at the muscled grace of movements. The memory of those hands against her skin. Yet something else she was losing.

Squeezing her eyes shut, she forced the thought away and turned her attention back to the world outside. She let herself get lost in the cabins with smoking chimneys that nestled into the mountainside.

Part of her still viewed things photographically, even if she'd given up the career hopes. How she would frame an image, capture the magic of a place. That kind of seeing never completely receded from her.

Despite the rising thud against her ribs, she imagined she might focus a camera on the red barn off in the distance. The foreground would feature the pinto horse that was bolting away from the barn, tail and mane streaming in the wind, floating across the cleared land, mountains suggesting freedom in the background.

It had been a long time since she'd followed through on those instincts, that part of her that recorded images freely. Lately, her photographs and documenting felt as hollow as the ache in her chest, maybe because the only photos she'd taken recently had been of the dairy farm for a file to pass to the inevitable Realtor to sell the property.

As the horse disappeared from view, swallowed by the trees, her attention snapped back to closer surroundings. A high-pitched laugh had Nina's head swiveling toward the back seat where the twins bounced with an excitement barely contained by the seat belt.

"I mean, just look at how beautiful the font is on this," Kelsey said, holding the "dog tag" the ranch sent three days prior. Her fingers traced her name. So like Kelsey—her attention to detail, to arrangement, made her a strong student.

"Who cares about the font?" Kacie scoffed, sliding the dog tag back and forth along the chain around her neck. "The engraving of the horse and running dog is basically the best part." Nina smiled, admiring the spirt Kacie possessed. Her interest in motion. The dog tags had arrived in the mail as part of their welcome package, the silver charms engraved with their names and parents' contacts in case they got separated.

A cute—and practical—gesture.

Gravel crunched beneath the truck tires as the woods became thicker, obscuring the sky with lithe limbs. A wooden porch on stilts peeked from trees with bright red leaves. Inviting and welcoming. The kind of place that housed laughter and smelled perpetually of baked goods—chocolate chip cookies and vanilla. Or at least, the glow of filtered sun on the pine-colored exterior certainly suggested that the cabin served such a purpose. She hadn't realized how much her soul craved an escape from the hardship of the farm until right this minute, looking at a creek gurgling and glistening in the late-day sun. A stone firepit, aged with time and smoke, invited from by the shore.

Her fingers itched to record every moment with her lens. And she would. But her children's need for peace had to come first.

Douglas steered the truck beside the cabin they'd been assigned and shifted the truck into Park. "All right, girls, let's unload."

Nina scooped her leather hobo bag from the floorboards. "We only have an hour before the welcome cookout for newcomers."

Her handsome husband took the steps up to the cabin in long, measured strides, stopping outside the door to punch in the code. He swung the door wide, holding it open for her; their eyes held as she angled past him, near enough to breathe in the familiar scent of his spicy aftershave.

Turning away from his still-alluring scent, she took in the details of the place they would call home for the next two weeks. Shiplap hugged the walls, framing the large stone fireplace that she was sure had chased the chill away from many Tennessee winter nights.

Ceiling beams added a touch of whimsy, complementing the wagon-wheel chandelier Douglas had just turned on. The light cast the cabin in a honey glow.

Peace must look like this. All warm and gathered beauty. She grazed her fingers along a wooden wall plaque. *Be the person your dog thinks you are.*

How would her dogs assess her now, she wondered? A failure?

The girls pitched their backpacks onto the leather sofa and climbed the ladder up to the loft, bunk bed visible. Puppy-paw patterns wandered across the two duvets. Complimentary cowboy hats rested on each pillow.

Her heart in her throat, she stepped into the master bedroom. A vintage claw-foot tub—perfect for soaking—took up the majority of the bathroom space.

Mimicking ivy and blossoming flowers, the wrought iron headboard and bed frame made the bed at once stately and romantic. "His" and "Hers" Stetsons were perched on the pillows.

Would she or Douglas take the plaid futon? Or would they ignore the futon and share the bed? They hadn't slept together in nearly six months. The sex between them had been dynamic, combustible, back in the day. Then it had become more of an exercise.

Then after their huge fight about closing the door to having more children, nothing at all.

Except in her memories. And those memories were so vivid, in weak moments, they made her long for something, anything from their relationship.

His shadow stretched past her and she didn't have to look over her shoulder to know he was there, so close, his breath whispered over her neck.

"I'll sleep on the sofa," he said softly, his voice warm and gravelly, like whiskey on the rocks.

"Don't be ridiculous." She stepped away, deeper into the room, keeping her back to him. "There's no need for you to wreck your back."

"Are you offering to sleep on the sofa or share the bed with me?"

She pivoted on her heels, crossing her arms against the temptation to say yes. "We've shared a room for longer than two weeks before without sleeping together. I think I can resist for the next fourteen days regardless of who rests their head on which pillow."

He chuckled wryly. "You always did know how to cut me down to size."

"At least I'm getting a reaction of some sort," she couldn't resist snapping back, only to regret the vulnerable words the second they left her mouth.

"Lady, you always get a reaction from me."

She exhaled long, hard, and sagged to sit on the end of the bed. "I'm too weary to play word games with you today."

"I thought we were calling a truce." He slid his fingers along a lock of her hair. "For now, anyway. We're here to let this place help us find a way through with our girls."

"Well, the girls have already informed me they want to attend the session on 'Pawsitivity.' I told them I was signing them up for 'To Furgive and Furget.'"

His low chuckle rumbled through the space as he stashed their suitcases in the closet. "We could probably lead a whole day on 'When Times Get Ruff.'"

"Too bad we didn't have a place like this years ago. I was so naive in thinking we would never need help." Nina swallowed a swell of regret and draped her jean jacket over a hook. She squinted to look closer at the photographs of Tennessee mountains dressed in summer green on a gallery wall.

"There was a time I knew exactly what you were thinking. All I had to do was look at your photos. Then you stopped showing me any of your pictures, and I was left clueless. Your face is far less telling."

"I could say the same about you."

"I'm not trying to keep secrets," he said, even though his face was a blank as ever. "I don't have any to keep."

"Oh, Douglas," she sighed, wishing she could make him understand in this rare pocket of opportunity when he was actually talking, communicating something more than just dry facts. "That's what make things even harder for the two of us. These days there's just…silence."

Except the feelings inside her were anything but quiet. She felt on fire with regrets and ache over those lost dreams. Over so much loss. She wanted to rage and scream. Except he would just shut down even more. If possible.

Resigned, she hugged her arms tight over her chest. "Could you check on the girls? I need to change for dinner."

What she really needed? A bath in that claw-foot tub to cover the sounds of a good cry.

Kelsey didn't feel at all like eating.

Her stomach churned with nerves as she trailed behind her family on their way to the welcome dinner. She really would have rather stayed in the cabin for a while since they weren't fighting for once. But she didn't get a say in much that went on in her life. She did better when she used her smarts to maneuver things the way she wanted them to happen. Like making this trip to the Top Dog Dude Ranch happen.

Except she hadn't thought beyond arriving. And what if it failed?

It couldn't. The place was too perfect to fail.

Tapping her leg in time with the banjo music, she scanned the cookout, which looked fun, with an Old West vibe. The spread of food was pressed up against the back of the lodge on a wooden patio, a vine-draped awning overhead. A covered wagon wheel held drinks labeled sweet tea, water, lemonade.

A red-checked tablecloth with a burlap runner hugged the packed table. Her stomach eased enough that her mouth started watering for the corn bread, biscuits, corn on the cob, slaw and barbecue. Lantern lights twinkled above her favorite—macaroni and cheese. Except she wasn't sure she would be able to eat anything.

She took an unsure step forward, being careful not to get so far back that her parents stopped talking to look for her, but not getting so close they spoke to her instead. So far, so good. Even Kacie was cooperating, more interested in looking at the grazing horses than in causing trouble. Kelsey scanned the group for allies, just like the heroine in her favorite mystery series would do. She needed grown-ups who understood her objective.

Other new arrivals approached her parents, extending hands to shake. She blinked in surprise. A wife pushed her husband in a wheelchair, a calico cat in his lap.

A hand rested on Kelsey's shoulder. She jolted, glanced back, and found a dark-haired lady with a name tag that said Hollie. "Could I help you find something? We don't want anyone to get lost."

She shook her head. "I'm okay. Just watching everyone." She held up her dog tag. "I'm Kelsey."

"Ah, I remember you from your letter. Such a smartly worded email. I can tell you're a good student." Hollie pointed to the man holding the cat. "Did you know there's a scientific reason that petting a cat is so soothing?"

"Seriously?" She stopped walking, intrigued that finally someone was speaking her academic language. She glanced back to check on her parents and they were standing close enough together she could take a minute to enjoy herself.

"Very seriously. A cat purrs at a frequency of around thirty hertz. That's right around the same frequency that stimulates tissue regeneration."

She frowned skeptically. "You're making that up."

"Not at all. It's one of the miracles of nature we utilize here at the Top Dog Dude Ranch."

"It's a miracle and it's science all at the same time."

"Exactly. People who let the animals follow their hearts will feel the healing boost."

She wished Kacie could understand this, too. It seemed like she should, given how much she loved horses. Maybe… "We have a cat named Waffles but he would rather play with my sister than sit in my lap while I study." Kacie was more fun. "Are there other miracles your animals do that are science, too?"

"Riding horses is therapeutic. And using the senses while riding helps a person process emotions."

Her gaze skipped over to Kacie stroking a horse's chestnut-colored forelock over the split-rail fence. "Like my sister would rather ride a horse and I want to cuddle the cat."

The lady's smile grew, her blue eyes sparkling. "That's a mature insight." She nodded back to the couple with the cat. "He was a firefighter. He and his fiancée are here to recover from a particularly terrifying scare."

His fiancée held his other hand, her brown skin glowing in the golden sunset. They seemed happy.

Maybe she could get her parents to hang out with them. Maybe that would rub off.

And maybe there were more allies to be found.

Kelsey pointed to the trio of women in line ahead of her sister. “What about them?”

The three looked related, like a grandma with a silver ponytail, a mom wearing a headscarf and granddaughter with a long, fat braid.

“The mother just beat cancer,” Hollie whispered. “Their trip here is their celebration.”

Kelsey’s stomach flipped, her limbs and heart heavy. Images of Uncle Tyler packed her head. Some from photos and some from memories. Her mom said they’d thought the worst had happened when he had his aneurysm, only to find out it was actually yet to come.

What if they could have brought him here? Even if he couldn’t be cured by the doctors, at least he could have had some help dealing with how sad he was. Her eyes stung, the party going blurry.

A whistle pierced the air.

Hollie leaned down. “That’s my husband’s way of saying he’s ready to welcome everyone. I should go join him.”

The ranch owner offered a big wave, holding his buff-colored Stetson in his hand. Lines crinkled around his eyes. “Welcome to the Top Dog Dude Ranch. I’m Jacob O’Brien, and this lovely lady…" He gestured to the woman at his side, her jeans and red plaid shirt matching her husband's. "This is my wife, Hollie."

If he was that old and still with his wife, he probably knew a thing or two about helping couples connect. Kelsey made a mental note to talk to him later. For now, she tuned in to what he had to say, careful to catch every word.

"We founded the Top Dog Dude Ranch with the mission that it would be more than a vacation spot. We wanted to create a haven, a place of refuge with tools available to help enrich your life. It's our hope that you carry a piece of the Top Dog experience with you."

Smoothing the sable vest over her red plaid shirt, Hollie smiled brightly. She reminded Kelsey of her teacher before the pandemic shut down their school. The kind of adult that made you feel like they'd give you a warm hug.

Moving closer to her husband, Hollie swept back her dark ponytail. "If you came here with burdens on your heart, we hope that your time here will do more than refresh you. But that you'll also find peace."

He slung an arm around his wife's shoulders as he continued, "And if you're wondering where to start, during breakfast tomorrow there will be a newcomers' session to acquaint you with the many options available at our ranch."

"Breakfast?" Kacie muttered under her breath to Kelsey. Getting up early didn't sound like a vacation to her. But she needed to remember she was here for her mom and dad. Kelsey elbowed her, shushing, and pointing to Mr. O'Brien finishing up his talk.

"We're especially excited that your two-week stay will wrap up with our annual Harvest Festival that's open to the public. There will be games and a parade. We finish off with a costume party for our guests. But for now—" the ranch owner gestured wide "—let's enjoy some of Tennessee's best barbecue."

A cheer lifted from the crowd as the guests started filing over, her parents moving toward the end of the line. She saw her dad gesture for her mom to go ahead of him. A good thing. But they didn't touch at all. And that worried her. Why didn't her dad even try?

She looked around at the other families there and her chest ached. She'd tried so hard to be good and not cause trouble, get good grades, do her chores, cover up what was really going on.

Kacie tugged her arm impatiently. "Quit daydreaming and come on, we're supposed to be acting like a family."

She couldn't let them guess. It wasn't easy for her, trying to pretend all the time, and she was so mad at Kacie for focusing on the stupid competition back home instead of helping more with getting their parents to stay together. Time was running out to repair their family.

Because if everything she'd studied up on was true, then before long, she would die just like her uncle.

Chapter Four

Douglas tucked his arm under his head and stared up at the shadows playing off the cabin ceiling. The futon wasn't half bad.

For a futon.

He would rather be in bed with his wife. In his bed at home. He needed to focus on this two-week window of time with no distractions.

Although she was a distraction of a whole other kind. Douglas drank in Nina's moonlit curves. Even from under the flowered quilt, she still could snatch his breath from his chest.

Scrubbing a hand over his bleary face, he gave up on sleep. He'd already called to check on the place three times, but even hearing that all was well didn't stop the worries, and yes, even the resentment over losing what could be the final days to enjoy his birthright.

One that had been hard-won. Filled with pain and resilience.

His dad had worked endlessly trying to save their land during a time when family-owned farms were struggling, then had a stroke in the field, dead before anyone found him. Their mom had died of a broken heart. Well, technically, it had been an overdose of her mood meds. He didn't think it had been intentional, more of a passive suicide.

Tyler had stepped up to take care of him at a time his brother had every right to lose himself in his own grief. He'd even left college, giving up his baseball scholarship. Been the model older brother. Sacrificed everything for him.

He'd been the one to teach Douglas how to fish, how to ask a girl out on a date. He'd encouraged Douglas to have a life other than the farm. But Douglas loved the land like his father had. It was in his blood.

Now he had no idea what to do with his life. The future looked so bleak without his home… his family.

It was such a simple house, but it was everything to him. It hurt to think how little it would sell for. Chances were that if the land sold, the house would be leveled.

The single-story brick ranch-style house was where he'd hung out in the kitchen with his mother. At first, he'd resented having to help cook, even if she was making his favorite, fried catfish. That was until his mother started telling stories of her childhood, of their family. How his grandmother had taught her all the family recipes in the way recipes used to be taught. Gathering around the stove, learning to cook by smell and color. A tradition he'd kept alive with Nina and the girls.

Then there was his family's sprawling red barn where he and Tyler had readied for a rodeo as kids. He and Tyler, armed with scissors, had approached Whisper, the red roan gelding. Horses needed their manes in tight braids for the show. So they'd tried their best, which had meant cutting the mane to only two inches. Completely unbraidable, but short. Mission half achieved. Phantom laughter ached in his gut as he remembered Tyler's wide-eyed surprise that their trimming efforts had resulted in something more like a horse mullet.

The memories were invaluable, but not particularly marketable. The milking machines and the cattle were the most valuable assets, yet once they were sold, there would be no way to keep the land

and have it turn a big enough profit to fight off the creditors.

Frustrated, he scrubbed a hand over his chest. Songs from owls and crickets filtered into the cabin as he tried to determine if her breathing was the slow, deliberate march of a dreamer. Or if she, too, found sleep impossible.

"Nina, are you awake?"

Blond hair awash in moonglow, she turned to him for a moment. Eyes meeting. A slight electric hum between them. Even in subdued light, her brown eyes warmed him.

Short-lived electricity crackled before she turned back to stare up at the ceiling "Yeah. Just thinking about that time we went to the Dresdyn Family Farm Festival five years ago. How Kacie ran into the corn maze chasing that border collie."

Memories of Kacie flickered through his head, his daughter ever impulsive and full of spirit, running in her dusty-pink cowgirl boots, blond hair streaming behind her. "I had forgotten about that. You know, I think that was the first night she picked up a rope."

Nina chewed her bottom lip as she did when lost in thought. "And Kelsey wanted the pumpkin patch attendant to explain what made some pumpkins grow so big and others so small. She was entranced by the variegated colors on some."

"Her curiosity is still insatiable." He sat up on the futon, playing with one of the dog-themed throw pillows, tossing it back and forth from hand to hand. "And then that rainstorm came and soaked us all to the bone. I was basically a drowned rat."

Laughing, she raised her hands to her face, fingers on her temple. "I remember the rainstorm, all right. But I also seem to remember that even though you were drenched, I pulled you to me, and we danced to that local band underneath the tent."

That night, she'd looked so beautiful in her jean shorts and tank top, was still so gorgeous it made his chest ache to know she was all his. He'd known even then that he'd been lucky to have her. "Nina?"

She didn't answer, or even look at him. But he saw her swallow as the memory clearly grabbed hold of her, too.

Douglas cleared his throat and tried a different approach. If farm life had taught him anything, it was to be flexible. To shift tactics to address the needs and demands of the land. That line of thinking seemed applicable here when so much was at stake between them. "You seemed to enjoy yourself tonight."

Dressed in shadows, her turn toward him

set something ablaze in him. All those years he thought they'd have to get it right.

"I did." She shifted under the covers. "It was fun chatting with the other couples."

"We haven't had much time for a social life over the years, first with preemie twins..." A lump lodged in his throat thinking of how close his daughters had come to dying, of living through the horror of waking up every morning wondering if they would still be alive when he put his head back on the pillow. He pushed through. "Then because of Tyler."

Except he didn't want to think of his brother right now. Nina would probably say he was pushing aside his emotions, but so be it. That was how he got through his days.

Sitting up in the bed, she hugged her knees, the light pink spaghetti-strap sleep shirt sliding down her shoulder. "It's nice to give the girls this break."

Their eyes met. Held. But then she shook her head as she looked away.

"And you," he pressed. "I'm glad *you* are getting this break."

"This trip doesn't change things between us."

He could sense her walls going up as tangibly as if they'd been built a brick at a time. He saw the way her jaw worked into a mask of ironed neutrality. No. Not neutrality. Something else… something more like a castle preparing for a siege.

And maybe in a way, the kingdom really was at stake. He needed to convince her that he wasn't the enemy. He wasn't a raider or a threat. So he would shift, make the space before them more comfortable. Anything to keep the line of dialogue open.

Maybe he needed to start talking her language more, even if he didn't feel it. "Who says the trip has to change anything?"

Willing his body into a nonchalant shrug that he didn't feel, he shot a sidelong glance her way.

"I'm not sure what you mean." She let go of her knees, straightening her legs and her spine. Alert.

Yes. He had her attention.

"What if we just roll with the flow, enjoy the free vacation with our girls and each other?" He let his thoughts wander with possibilities of where this time could lead. What he wouldn't give for the chance to hold her again. Touch her. Remind her how good they could be together. Fairy-tale love wasn't everything. Their life together—and yes, the passion they felt for each other—was more than enough, more than many people had.

Nina tilted her head. "What exactly do you mean by 'enjoy'?"

He was glad the dark covered his smile. "Nothing more and nothing less than what you want it to mean."

Her husky laugh flowed over him. "Somehow I doubt you can keep to that vow."

And she would be right.

"I'll take that as a challenge."

"Really?" she asked warily.

"Absolutely. I'll keep things platonic..." Hopefully not for much longer, he thought. "Although you can feel free to change the rules anytime."

He waited, but the silence stretched. "Nina, do we have a deal to go with the flow?"

"And I can really trust you to keep your word?"

"Have I ever lied to you?" He may have messed up his fair share of things in the past, but he kept his word.

"No, Douglas, you are a man of honor."

Was that why even the thought of divorce was beyond considering? He didn't shirk responsibility. "All right, then. What's on the agenda for tomorrow?"

"The girls are choosing, and they didn't say other than they want to surprise us." She stretched back out again. "We should get some sleep or we'll be dead to the world in the morning."

Sleep? Not likely. After a conversation that opened up the possibility of touching her again, he would have to be dead to sleep when the wife he hungered for was just a few short steps away.

Nina couldn't remember when she'd last felt so alive.

She told herself that had nothing to do with the conversation she'd had with Douglas the night before, even if the idea of spending the next two weeks together away from the stresses of home was becoming more and more tempting. So much so, it was all she could do not to reach out to him now.

Settling into the saddle, her fingers resting on the well-worn leather of the horn, she adjusted her weight to the white mare's leisurely gait. Hands loose on the rein braids. Barely having to guide the mare, Moonbeam, as she rode beside her husband and fell in line behind the ranch guests, about a dozen in all, some of whom she'd met at the cook-out the night before.

The early-morning sun sent dappled beams through the trees along the grandmother, mother and daughter trio, sitting atop big, beautiful bay horses, their black manes and tails streaming in the light breeze that rustled the trees as they made their way into a more shaded portion of the mountain trail. From where Nina rode, she could feel the intergenerational connection between the women.

And something in her heart broke a bit at the lack of connection in her own life.

No matter. She would stay here. Present in the golden glow of a Tennessee fall, her breath puffing clouds in the cold morning air. The smell of damp leaves and steady sounds of hoofbeats on loose dirt.

True, they lived on a farm. True, Archer land was lovely. But she couldn't remember the last time she had spent time outside like this, experiencing rather than working. Had allowed herself to take in such pristine beauty. To really just be present.

At the very head of the line, Jacob turned in his saddle. The ranch owner surveyed the line, ensuring no one had gotten lost.

She registered every nuance with her artistic eye, taking advantage of the horse's steady gait to lift the camera and snap photos. Tufts of silver-gray smoke rose from a cabin that seemed to melt into the landscape. Swishing tails. Leaves on the oaks the colors of fire, of change. Birdsong. A doe peering from behind bark, those dark eyes deep and knowing, unafraid of the group as they passed by. Snippets of conversation and hoofbeats folding into a sweet melody.

Her love of photography had grown as a teen, taking photos in each foster home, hoping to hold on to a sense of family, home, love, before she lost it again. As inevitably happened. How ironic that when she put down the camera, thinking she was safe, she actually lost everything.

She pushed away the negative thought and focused on the moment.

Again turning in his saddle, the reins easy in his left hand, Jacob O'Brien raised his right hand, pointing down the valley's ridge. "That's our little Top Dog village, modest but full of the best people you'll meet."

He directed their attention down the clusters of red, yellow and orange trees toward the tiny community. Several shops leaned against each other, the street small and quaint. A carryover, she guessed, from the turn of the twentieth century.

"The building in the center is Hollie's ice cream shop. You won't find a creamier selection around." He angled a glance back at Nina and Douglas. "Although I would imagine your dairy farm offerings might give us a run for our money when it comes to fresh ice cream."

What would life be like without the things she'd taken for granted? Fresh milk, farm eggs, ice cream made from the very best milk their cows had to offer?

Without Douglas?

She shot a glance at her husband, who was looking too sexy for his own good. How did he manage to make a beat-up jean jacket over flannel so mouthwateringly masculine? The sherpa collar was flipped up against his neck, no doubt catching against the bristles of his unshaven face. Her fingers twitched at the phantom memory of the texture.

Jacob continued, "It's hard to see from here, but it'll get easier as we keep heading north. There is a cave with hot springs that our patrons can schedule times to indulge."

"Wait a second," Kelsey squealed.

"What is it, darlin'?" Jacob asked, concern shadowing his eyes. "Are you feeling uncomfortable on Lyra?"

She shook her head. "I'm fine, thanks."

Kacie stroked the sorrel mane of her horse, Jupiter. "That's just what she does when she gets excited or remembers something."

Delight and possibilities colored Kelsey's blue eyes deeper. "Are those the hot springs that are called Sulis Springs? As in the place where magic carried from the Old World still lives with the animals who lived nearby?"

The ranch owner nodded. "Someone has been doing their homework. Yes, this is Sulis Springs. Once upon a time, when my ancestors were settling in this area from Scotland and Ireland, they followed a doe to the cave opening. It wasn't just any old doe, though. So, Kelsey, did your research tell you that as well?"

"It was the Queen of the Forest—who glowed like starlight, right?" She all but bounced in the saddle as she answered.

"That's right. The Queen of the Forest. My ancestors knew the type of animal well. They used to roam Scotland and lead wayward souls to safe places and healing water. They offered respite. A way to connect. You see, my ancestors were struggling to get settled in this region. Many challenges almost broke them. They wanted to give up on the land. On each other. But they followed the Queen of the Forest to the cave mouth."

Nina's stomach clenched. She could all but feel the weight of Douglas's gaze. No doubt he identified with the O'Brien passion for land.

Kacie leaned imperceptibly forward in her saddle.

Jacob clasped the reins loosely in his hands. "There was a lost pup in the cave that needed attention. So while they waited for a pot of coffee to brew over the fire, they cleaned up the young pup. As they rinsed the puppy, their bond was renewed. Healed. They found a way to work with the land, with one another."

Kelsey leaned to whisper to her mom, "See, I told you. Magic."

"Now," Jacob finished up his tale, "for the past couple centuries, people take the same path back to the Sulis Springs and leave pumpkins and fresh-cut sunflowers for the Queen of the Forest and her magic that brings people together. Much like how our hot springs have healed and gathered people to this land for over a hundred years. We have a reputation for bringing people together because of it."

Jacob nodded toward a small pond a hundred yards down the hillside, his brown Stetson obscuring his eyes for a moment. Rustling autumn wind stirred a simple, lacy white wedding gown on a woman in her midfifties. The groom, silver-haired, clasped his bride's hands as he stood on the dock by the pond.

"Those two came to the ranch last year, separately. Rumor has it they fell for each other when he jumped into the pond to save her."

Kelsey gasped. "What happened to her?"

"A fish hopped into her canoe, startling her dog, which tipped over the boat." He pointed. "That same dog is their ring bearer."

For heartbeats that felt like centuries, Nina's eyes followed the scene unfolding on the dock. The sparse but beautiful flowers. Sparkling flecks of water. So enchanted by the scene, she'd fallen out of her place in the trail line. Awareness of Douglas pulsed through her as Moonbeam's stride became even more leisurely. Nina hadn't even realized their horses were trailing the others. She glanced at Douglas suspiciously.

In the morning sunlight, Douglas's blue eyes held the mischief and delight that had first pulled her into his orbit. Broad, muscled shoulders tempered by all that work on their farm. As handsome today as he'd been on their wedding day. Such a blur. So different from the calm scene unfolding on that valley-side pond. He'd been in a sharp tux, bolo tie and black Stetson, young and full of dreams. Simmering with sleek, sexy muscles and high-cut cheekbones that always made him seem he was in the middle of a great discovery.

"Our wedding day was such chaos," she mused softly, careful to keep her voice low enough that their children wouldn't overhear and misconstrue.

Hands sliding on the reins, he nudged his black gelding to stay on the trodden trail. Those eyes—blue as the innermost part of a flame—locked with hers. "I don't remember it that way."

She couldn't hold back a laugh. "Because a man just has to show up."

"Fair enough. I wouldn't have noticed chaos anyway. I was in the barn with Tyler working a surprise delivery of twin calves."

"I remember those twins. I thought the vet came out for that."

Douglas shook his head. "Old Doc Gerald arrived too late for the actual birth and just did the exams afterward. I didn't want to stress you. You had enough on your plate getting dressed for the wedding."

She mulled that over for a moment as the rest of the group moved on, leaving her and Douglas trailing behind.

"We've always done that, haven't we? Kept things to ourselves so as not to worry the other. I wonder if we'd been more open, if…"

"If what?" he asked, his strong hands loose on the reins.

"If it might have eased the stress, sharing the burdens."

His grip tightened ever so slightly, and for a moment she thought he would press the advantage, in spite of his promise to go with the flow. Her heart sped in her chest; her breath caught in her throat. She could see the widening of his pupils, familiar, heated.

Then he stroked along the brim of his Stetson and trained his eyes forward. "I guess we'll never know."

She should be relieved he kept his word. But

she couldn't help wondering what she would have done if he'd angled in to kiss her.

There were few things as anchoring to Douglas as watching folks move in time together in a line dance. An upbeat song bringing the barn together, laughing faces after a full day of sunlit adventure atop horses.

And tonight's "Boot Scootin' Boogie" had set the barn alive.

He scanned the other guests in their array of denim and flannel, some with sleeves rolled up in spite of the slight briskness in the evening air sweeping in through the wide-open doors. The darting of his children drew his eyes, Kacie picking up the dance quickly, her natural athleticism serving her well tonight, just as it did when roping. Kelsey stood slightly out of line, brow furrowed, assessing each new movement before entering.

Finally, he let his gaze settle on his wife. She stretched her hand back directing Kelsey subtly. Graceful as though she were directing a symphony. A black off-the-shoulder cable-knit sweater hugged the curves on her body. Accentuating her beautiful smile. Blond hair loose, falling in pools on her bare shoulders.

A hand clapped him on the back and he turned to find the ranch owner.

"How are you enjoying the place so far?"

Looking beneath the twinkling lights, the silhouette of the mountains beyond, he had to admit there was something…different about this place. Something he couldn't quite name, but that drew him in. "It's quite a spread you have here."

"I was surprised to see your application, given you have much the same to offer at your farm. Most folks come here as a total change of pace from their everyday life."

"My girls chose. They heard about the famed magic of the Top Dog Dude Ranch." The planked floor groaned beneath his feet as he shifted, taking in the gathered group.

Jacob tipped back his Stetson. "Well, I do have to say it was the craziest timing in the world to see your request come in. We usually book months in advance. We had a cancellation five minutes before we opened the email with your reservation request."

"I'm glad for my girls." A tightness in his chest gnawed at him.

"That's not all. The family that canceled—a family of four—wouldn't take the refund, even though we told them we had a waiting list. They insisted that their prepayment be donated to another family."

Douglas scratched the back of his neck. "That's what I heard. I still can hardly believe it."

"The timing was definitely kismet, and it had nothing to do with the animals."

"Our girls wanted to come so much they were raising money to come here, but there's no way they could have gotten even close."

A wide grin stretched across Jacob's weathered face. "Thanks for sharing that story. Affirmation like that means a lot. We're packed, but times haven't always been easy, especially during all the virus shutdowns."

Douglas scratched the side of his neck right over a crick that had been there for longer than he could remember. "We were hit hard as well, losing contracts for milk and beef."

"Oh, man, that's rough. I saw stories about dairy farms having to pour out gallons of milk."

"Our town is small. There wasn't much of a safety net for a lot of folks. My wife came up with a plan for us to give it away." He looked at Nina, so alive and giving.

"Give away the milk and beef?"

"She said it seemed wasteful not to." And she'd been right. He'd had such tunnel vision he'd missed what should have been obvious. Nina probably understood well from her upbringing what it was like to struggle financially; even when her parents had been alive, money was tight. So she never missed a chance to give someone a hand up when it was within her means. "My wife said she figured even if someone had plenty of money, this would free up more for them to do for someone else."

"She sounds like a good person."

"Yes, she is." His eyes were drawn to Nina, to what coming here could mean. To his last hope for bringing his family together. "Some of those folks are taking care of our home and animals while we're here. I'm going to miss that small-town connection when we move."

Jacob arched an eyebrow. "Move? Where to?"

"We're putting the place on the market when we get back. We haven't told the girls. We wanted to give them this chance to be carefree first."

And that was the last thing he needed to be talking about if he wanted to keep this vacation lighthearted. "Forget I said anything."

"Hey, this may be a bit out of the blue, but if you do decide to sell, how about give me a call. We've been looking for land to expand, open a second ranch, and I'd like to take a look at your operation."

"Thanks, I'll keep that in mind," he said automatically. He should be shouting for joy over even the possibility. But he just felt hollow.

Quick beats of the line dance receded. In their stead, a soulful fiddle was joined by a crooning voice. Now this was his moment. He said his goodbye to Jacob and took sure-footed steps toward Nina.

He touched the soft fabric at her elbow. Imagining already what it'd be like to touch her. To be close to her. "May I have this dance?"

Her eyes went wide and hesitant. Which made him all sorts of sad.

"Nina, for the girls. For the vacation." He held out his arms.

Thank God, she didn't leave him standing there like a fool. She stepped forward and finally, *finally*, he had his wife in his arms, her hair flying behind her with each swing, her cheeks flushed and her eyes alive.

In the warm glow of lights strung overhead, her brown eyes glistened, her breath whispering across his skin as a twirl landed her close to his cheek. "I forgot you could dance like this."

"I believe I forgot as well. But it feels good to see you smile."

"Keep dancing and I'll keep right on smiling, cowboy."

If only it could be that simple.

He felt the electricity hum in the rapidly diminishing space between them. Lips so close as they passed, heat and fire in their gaze. Need rose in his chest with each ragged breath.

A fat gray tabby pressed against his legs and hers, seeming to push them closer and closer. Until they were seconds, a mere breath away. And then she swayed into him, only a hint, but all the encouragement he needed to capture her lips.

Chapter Five

The familiar press of her husband's mouth to hers built a longing in her for more than sex.

Strains of the country band still teasing her ears, Nina swayed into the solid breadth of his chest, hard muscles from real work and a lifetime of it. He stirred a desire for what they'd once shared and everything they'd dreamed of becoming. Of the life they'd imagined building together.

Chemistry had never been their problem. In fact, they'd likely relied too heavily on letting it bridge difficult times, especially after his brother died. Those moments of being connected were often the only outlet for emotion. Or rather, the only outlet for Douglas. She'd craved those moments of connection. Even though Tyler wasn't her biological relative, she'd had such little family in her life, his death hit her hard as well.

And oh, as her fingers twisted in the warm flannel of her husband's shirt, how she wanted to indulge in one last night with him, to pretend this place really could work magic and their problems would all disappear. Her skin tingled at the possibility, a sigh sliding free.

Her lashes fluttered and she caught sight of her daughters in the distance. Seeing their wide and hopeful eyes iced her heated blood.

"Douglas," she whispered against his lips, now all too aware of the other dancers swaying around them. "The girls are watching and we don't want to mislead them."

A tic twitched at the corner of his eye. "Of course. You're right. I don't imagine I could persuade you to take a stroll in the moonlight?"

Then he smiled and winked.

Heaven help her, when he smiled her insides turned to mush as they always did in his rare shows of humor. The first time he'd laughed, she'd lost her heart. She couldn't even remember now what it was that spurred him. Just that they'd been walking by the farm's pond and she'd cracked a joke, nothing special, but he'd made her feel important. Something she hadn't felt in such a long time.

Definitely no romantic moonlight walks.

"It's getting late." She backed away, bumping into an older couple. "Excuse me."

Douglas braced her by the elbow, his touch strong and warm. "The girls are having fun. What harm is there in letting them have a good time? We both know farm life is hard work. They deserve to be kids."

He had chosen now to be chatty? Now? After she'd begged him for over a year for more than clipped sentences?

Well, too little, too late. A whisper was all she could muster as the weight of her words tumbled from her lips. "You're right that this is about the kids, not us, not having a vacation or 'going with the flow.' Am I wrong?"

His jaw flexed, tensing, his lips thinning. That's what she'd thought. Short-lived levity.

She angled past him, waving to the twins, who thank goodness, didn't seem to have overheard. "Come on, girls. We have an early day tomorrow."

As a careful student of photography, Nina knew how to pose her body to convey emotion and outline feeling. Even when the emotions didn't match the exterior gestures.

Which is exactly what she did now—forced

and willed her body into a jovial dance her bones detested as she gathered their children, with a slightly rickety smile.

Snatching her jean jacket from the row of hooks by the barn door, she stuffed her arms inside without pausing and stepped out into the crisp evening air.

What had she been thinking? How could she have let herself get so carried away? She didn't have the luxury of a moment's weakness with her husband. This trip was about preparing the girls for a split. Not for getting their hopes up, which would make the fall all the harder.

Time to shore up her defenses and stay focused on forging a future for herself and the girls.

Douglas jolted in his bed, expecting morning but only finding moonbeams.

He'd always been a light sleeper, first keeping an ear open for problems on the farm, and then for sounds that his brother might need him. And even half-awake, his honed senses told him there was something on the move in their cabin.

A critter?

Thump.

There it was again.

He swung his legs off the futon, the quilt gathering around his waist. Quietly, he tugged on a

T-shirt, stealing a quick glance at his wife. She still slept, her breaths even.

She hadn't said two words to him since storming out of the barn dance. But he wasn't letting that deter him, especially after that kiss they'd shared. Surely she'd only been riled up because she'd felt the heat simmering right along with him. She'd needed to shut him down afterward because she didn't know what to do with all those feelings. He understood. And he would wait. He was a patient man and now that he'd seen her wavering, he'd had his first taste of hope in a long, long time.

Easing the bedroom door open, he found…

The last thing he expected.

Kacie stood in the middle of the room, the wagon-wheel chandelier on dim, swishing the lasso over her head. Tossing. Rolling the rope back in. Repeating. Hitting her target about half the time. A chair. A shoe. Her backpack. On and on. So engrossed, she didn't even seem to know he'd entered the room.

Barefoot, she wore pink thermal pj's. Her hair straggled down her back in a long, messy braid that always managed to come loose seconds after her mom had cinched it with a rubber band.

Her concentration was fierce, admirable, but her arm was starting to slide, clearly from exhaustion. In the top bunk just barely visible in the loft, her sister slept on. Had Kelsey grown used to the late-night practice sessions? He shook his head, all too aware that he hadn't spent enough time with his daughters in the last months of nonstop work. One of many problems he would start fixing this week.

"Hey, Champ, what are you doing still awake?"

The rope dropped from Kacie's hands, thudding to the floor. "Dad, I didn't hear you. I'm just getting in some practice for the festival championships when we get home. This is my year." Her chin went tight. "It has to be."

Placing a hand on her shoulder, he gave a gentle squeeze. He understood this dedication, the way it could swallow a person whole. The exact opposite of what he wanted for his daughter.

"Kacie, do you know what it means when a person talks about the point of diminishing returns?"

"Um, not really."

"It's when you work too long at something until you're so tired that instead of learning anything, you start to get worse."

"Are you saying I'm bad?" Tears glinted in her eyes and she scrubbed them away impatiently with the back of her hand.

"No, not at all. But you need to know when to stop a training session. Practice is important, but skills can't be fast-tracked. Does that make sense?"

Moonlight threw shadows and light playing hide-and-seek across her face as she chewed her lip. Exhaling hard, she rolled the lasso between thumb and forefinger.

"I think so."

"You're incredible, much better than I was at your age."

"Really?" A cousin to Tennessee starlight shone in her eyes.

"Absolutely. I would never lie to you." He nodded. Honesty had been his signature parenting style.

She snorted, avoiding his eyes.

Douglas frowned. She was spunky, but she had never been disrespectful. "Kacie, what's that supposed to mean?"

"You and Mom aren't telling the truth to us."

That was a minefield he didn't want to venture into for her. And quite frankly, he didn't want to consider what it meant if she had a point. "About what?"

She scrubbed a bare toe against the braid rug. "You're getting a divorce, aren't you?"

His insides went still, quiet. This was not a conversation he wanted to have, especially without Nina present. He opted for a truthful answer that still dodged sharing too much. “We have not filed for a divorce.”

“But you’re planning to.” She clenched her fists at her side, stubborn jaw jutting. “I saw you two fight tonight.”

“Let’s enjoy the trip.”

She rolled up her rope with angry, jerky loops. She’d always been feisty, but since Tyler’s death, that spunk had turned to anger. It seemed she resented everything these days.

“Kacie?”

She stopped, keeping her back to him, her shoulders so thin and sagging. “What, Dad?”

“I love you, Champ. That’s never gonna change.”

She climbed the ladder, mumbling, “That’s what you told Mom.”

Her words stabbed him clean through and there wasn’t anything he could think to say that would reassure her. He would need Nina’s guidance on this, like he did anytime emotional issues arose. Nina would know what to do.

Too bad he didn’t have a mentor to help him sort through the mess he’d made with his wife.

The twins’ laughter carrying on the wind almost managed to distract Nina from her husband’s looming presence just behind her. Kacie and Kelsey dangled from the rock wall, an instructor beneath each of them. Notches had been cut into a stone mountainside, leading up about twenty feet, grips and hooks bolted in. Kacie had chosen this activity, and Nina had to agree the exercise's focus on cooperation was certainly needed.

If she weren't afraid of heights, Nina would dangle from that wall all day if there was a chance of gaining insights from that vantage point.

It made her think of her parents. For the most part, she preferred to stuff down the memories and forge ahead with life. Thinking about her folks just hurt too much. But truth be told?

She hated this time of year.

October skies carried Canada geese flying south in a vee. Each flap of a wing sent a silent shudder through the group. A reminder of the consequences of small gestures, little choices. The fleetingness of movement and life.

Like what had happened with her parents. Grief, even all these years later, had such a peculiar way of showing up—an uninvited houseguest burrowing down, down, down into her chest.

She swallowed a gulp of air before clenching her jaw. Before her thoughts drifted to that time when her world collapsed, when her parents died. Guilt rose in her breath as she trailed the geese in the sky, falling back to that moment when everything changed. To another sun-soaked day with blue skies and potential. She'd been looking forward to the day at the lake all week. Her parents had saved up to buy a boat, full of plans of all the dinners they would catch. She'd been careful to do her homework and her chores. She'd accepted a ride home from school with a friend so she could get a head start on packing.

Her mom had been angry in that quiet way that was somehow scarier than if she'd shouted. Nina wasn't supposed to take rides from people her parents hadn't met, and she definitely wasn't supposed to get in a car with anyone without contacting her parents about the change in plans.

She knew the rules. And she'd broken them. If she hadn't, she'd have been on the boat with her parents instead of grounded, being watched by a neighbor. She would have died, too. Or maybe they wouldn't have died at all.

Survivor's guilt was a heavy weight to carry. And how sad was it that on most days the way things ended eclipsed the good from all the years before?

Before her parents died—such a strange line to have in her life so young—there had been laughter in her household. Her mother would bake dozens of muffins every Easter. Cinnamon streusel, blueberry, lemon-poppy seed. Flavors of spring and new life, her father had said. They'd save about a dozen for themselves. But then they took muffins to neighbors and friends, sharing conversation in many households over coffee and tea and the simple act of offering food. And that tradition sank with the death of her parents. It had never been the same.

Traditions like that hadn't been a part of her foster homes, not with so many kids and so many life skills they had to learn by eighteen. And so a part of her had ceased to be after the boating accident. A line running through her life. Before and after.

And now? She felt queasy, imagining yet another before and after.

"Nina," Douglas whispered over her shoulder. "The girls are settled here for at least an hour. We need to talk about last night."

Talk? Alone? Nope. "It was a kiss, Douglas, nothing more."

"That's not what I mean." He looked around. "And I don't want the girls to see us arguing. Let's step outside."

She hesitated.

"Nina, I wouldn't ask if it wasn't important." He splayed his arms wide. "I'll keep my hands to myself. Promise."

"Fine, ten minutes, though. Then we need to

get back to the girls. They're really excited about goat yoga later today—that was Kelsey's pick."

"Goat what?" He gestured her away from the rock wall and toward stepping-stones shaped like paws, leading toward a pond.

"You heard me. Goat yoga. Didn't you read the agenda Kelsey printed out for us?" Dew coated the grass, footfalls rustling as they walked toward the lily pad–covered pond.

He scrubbed a hand along the back of his neck. "I was a little late getting moving this morning."

She glanced sideways at him. "Yes, what was that all about? You never oversleep."

Lake-colored eyes, deep blue and serious, assessed her. "I found Kacie up in the great room in the middle of the night practicing her lassoing skills."

"Was she having trouble sleeping?" Nina took a seat on the wooden bench. "Was she working the lasso to soothe herself?"

"She looked dead exhausted on her feet. She said something about running out of time to win this year's festival competition."

"Okay, she's been wanting that for a while."

"Yeah, but she's afraid this year will be her last chance since we're moving." Sitting beside her, he leaned forward, forearms bracing on his knees. "She's guessed that we're getting a divorce."

Gasping, she gripped his arm. "What did you say?"

"I told her that we had not 'filed' for divorce and then tried to change the subject."

While she appreciated him not sharing that with their daughter, she also couldn't help but imagine him sidestepping the emotional conversation as he did so often. "I guess we haven't done as good a job at shielding them as we thought."

"Seems so." He looked at her sidelong beneath the brim of his Stetson, his eyes piercing…with a surprising flash of vulnerability. Even if she and Douglas still loved each other, their world would be changing forever once the farm was sold.

Initially, she and Douglas had been drawn to each other by their mutual loss, each understanding what it was like to lose parents so young. But he just didn't understand what it felt like to have no one, nowhere to go, no place to call home. In his grief, he'd had his brother and his childhood home, a home he would lose soon.

Her parents' assets had been sold off to pay off the hospital bills from the accident. Their home had been a rental. Everything she'd owned fit into an old beat-up suitcase and a big black garbage bag.

She scratched a hand along the ache in her ribs. "I hate this for the kids. I know what it's like to lose your home, your family. I guess I need to remind myself it's not like they're going into foster care."

Movement from the corner of her eye sent Nina's heart pounding. Water splashed from the pond, sailing over the low railing on the dock. Instinctively, she moved closer to Douglas. Whipping her head to the pond, she caught shimmered scales receding from view. Nerves quieted for a moment.

Until another awareness settled in. Douglas. So close she could feel the warmth move from his body to hers—a personal jet stream that brewed and calmed the storms churning in her soul.

She imagined the photograph they made right now. Her plaid shirt slightly wet, leaning imperceptibly closer than moments before. His tanned face and strong chest contrasting her curves. Yes, photography anchored her.

Her photos had been a way to find beauty in a world gone so very ugly.

"You've never talked much about that time in your life after your parents died."

She frowned. "I'm sure that's not true. We've been married for over a decade."

"You haven't." He went still. As if he was determining a path forward. So close. In a quiet voice, a gentle one she hadn't heard in some time, he pressed, "I may not talk as much as you would like, but I do listen, Nina."

"I know. I guess I'm more surprised at myself for not sharing more about my childhood." She searched her mind for something to dispute what he said, only to realize he was right. Had her pride in her ability to communicate been false pride? She'd shared her emotions, but so very little of what shaped her.

"Life has always been packed for us. It's easy to see how we just fell into bed at the end of the day."

Their eyes caught. Locked into place with a call and response. One she had trouble shifting away from. Part of her never wanted to stop looking into those eyes, noticing the way light set them ablaze. And chemistry was so much easier to focus on than her own shortcomings.

He rested a hand on the back of her neck, rubbing softly. "I'm sorry that foster care was so bad for you."

She cleared her throat. Even if she'd fallen short in the past, she could do better now. "Well, after three quick pit-stop placements, I actually landed with some good people, an older retired military couple. No cliché there." Her lips twitched with a half smile. "They took in a lot of us older kids. It was better than a group home, but still pretty packed." An especially tough transition for an only child. “Not a lot of emotional space to grieve for my parents.”

“They were taking in extra kids and pocketing money?”

“Not at all,” she rushed to explain. “We were each taught how to open a bank account and they deposited half the money there for us to learn to budget. The other half, they put into a savings account we were each given when we turned eighteen.”

“Wow, so they sound like special people.”

“That’s an understatement.” Truly. Things could have been so much worse and there was no gain for them other than giving teens a helping hand. “As long as we kept the grades up and followed the rules.”

“And if you didn’t?”

“Then money was deducted from the bank account and moved over to savings, since life was going to be harder at eighteen if we had crummy grades or got into trouble with the law.”

“I assume you behaved?” He stroked a lock of her hair.

“I did, and I was able to leave town for college. Ashlynn wasn’t as lucky.” Again, Nina wondered how she’d missed sharing this with her husband. Had they talked about anything of substance? “She got in trouble with the law.”

"Ashlynn got arrested? I can't imagine her doing something like that."

Down the dock, a fluffy white golden retriever let out a woof, drawing her attention away for a moment. Tail wagging, the dog started into a headlong run toward them, full of boundless puppy joy and energy.

Skidding to a stop, the golden retriever pranced over. Nudged Douglas's hand, demanding a proper head scratch, which he obliged.

"She wasn't an angel back in those days, so full of anger over the crap hand life had dealt her, but she didn't do anything extreme. She had a crush on a boy and did whatever it took to spend time with him, including skipping school. Some schools may be looking for other ways to deal with truancy these days. But back then? Not as much. She ended up in juvie."

"How awful. Was the guy just leading her on?"

"She wasn't wrong that he loved her, but he died in a DUI accident. She's still in the same town working at the same restaurant." With his tail wagging, lightly smacking Nina's jean-covered leg, the dog sat in the small space between them, like a sort of bridge connecting them. Unable to resist, she reached down to pet the silken dog.

"I know you care about her very much."

Her chest went tighter with more emotion than

even she cared to admit. The golden moved his head, causing her fingertips to slightly brush against the back of Douglas's hand. Heat rose in her as emotions rocked through her, unsteady waves of possibilities and dreams deferred, dreams broken. "It doesn't seem fair. I ended up throwing away my chance at college, too. I remind myself I have two amazing children and I wouldn't trade them for anything."

The golden adjusted, lying on her feet. She took a breath in as the dog's gentle presence soothed the tempest inside her. The one she couldn't let make landfall. Tears threatened but she felt them ebb with the steady heartbeat of the dog that grounded her.

Just as did the warm press of Douglas's leg against hers.

Douglas leaned forward. "And?"

Unable to resist, she stroked a hand along his jaw, soaking in the familiar feel of him. "I'm so sorry about Tyler and all that you've lost."

The warm bristle of his unshaved face rasped against her nerves, delicious, tempting. Touch had a way of igniting so much between them.

"I'm sorry I let you and the girls down."

She hated that he felt like a failure when she knew all too well how much of himself he'd poured into trying to save the farm. She especially hated that she couldn't figure out how to get them back to what they'd once had. But she was so very weary with carrying the whole relationship. Time after time when she or the girls needed comfort, or just to vent, he would find some task that needed doing around the farm. Their fence had been "repaired" so often he could have rebuilt the thing twice over.

Rising, she stepped back from her husband and the lure of whatever magic the ranch was trying to weave around them. "We should get back to the girls. This trip is for them, after all."

And she would do well to remind herself of that.

Chapter Six

How had he lost sight of the simple things in life?

A bonfire.

Dinner under the stars.

Having his family in one place.

Standing by the pit with massive flames shooting up from the wooden pyre, Douglas speared a hot dog onto a skewer for Kelsey. Kacie, of course, had insisted on making her own, half of which was about to fall off and into the fire. He could already imagine her declaring that's just what she intended.

Her independent streak would serve her well. She was a lot like her mom that way, even if folks assumed she was more like him because of her love for animals.

A fiddler sat on a bale of hay, filling the night air with old country tunes. About fifty guests gathered, scattered around, some sitting on wooden benches, others parked on blankets.

Crouching beside Kelsey, Douglas passed the skewer to her. “Here you go, Princess.”

“Thanks, Dad,” she said softly, more subdued than usual.

“Is everything okay? Do you feel all right?” He pressed his wrist to her forehead. “You don’t feel like you have a fever.”

She shook her head. “Don’t worry about me. I just need to eat some supper. Thanks for fixing this.” She grinned. “Mine will taste much better than Kacie’s burned and twisted hot dog. We should do this at home. Don’t you think?”

“Sure, kiddo. We’ll talk to your mom.”

Back when his parents had been alive, they’d hosted gatherings like this every week. Everyone would bring a side dish. Whoever played an instrument would strike up tunes.

He’d asked Tyler once if they could start the tradition back up again. Tyler had said it made him too sad—one of the few times he’d voiced his own grief.

Douglas hadn’t asked again.

Would Nina have been happier if he'd expanded their world more? She probably could have used another outlet during Tyler's illness. Especially when Douglas had struggled with handling the emotional stuff. He'd often wished her foster sister had lived closer to give Nina someone to talk to on a regular basis. Confide in.

At least here, now, he had a chance to find a way to rebuild and he intended to make the most of every opportunity.

He shifted to sit beside her on the quilt while keeping a watch over the twins standing at the outskirts of the fire. Nina hugged her knees, swaying to the music. Her golden-blond hair, gathered in a ponytail, swished along her back. The firelight threw a warm glow around her. She hummed along with the old folk song. Her voice wasn't pitch-perfect but sweet. Happy.

He'd missed her smile.

She tipped her face to him, her grin lighting all the way up to her eyes. "You were a good sport about goat yoga today."

"Well, it was certainly a new experience for me." Thanks to farm life, he'd spent plenty of time around goats. Milking them. Corralling them. Getting kicked by them. But he'd never held a baby goat while trying—unsuccessfully—to strike a tree pose.

Nina toyed with the end of her ponytail, playing with her hair as she did when nervous. "Thank you for going along with it. Kelsey was so very excited. And Kacie couldn't stop laughing at us."

"It was pretty funny when our goat bridge collapsed. I'm glad you took pictures at the end." Bleating goats with their rectangle-shaped pupils tumbling and arching in the air. Desperate to get away from the high-pitched laughter of Kacie and Kelsey. Even he and Nina had laughed from deep in their bellies. Rare. And utterly awesome. She took his breath away.

"How could I not take photos? That was definitely a unique opportunity."

Flickering warm light caught in her eyes like twinkling stars. Their gazes locked. Outside sounds were muffled as more than the fire sparked and danced in the small space between them.

He reached, watching for a sign of hesitation in her, and when finding none, he stroked down the length of her ponytail. Her hair had always been so impossibly soft, tempting, especially when brushing along his chest when she was on top. "It's been good for us to get away."

"You're right. It has."

Drawing waves in the dirt with the toe of his boot, he looked at her sidelong. "I'm sorry I haven't been better about finding time for R and R."

As his fingers entwined tighter around her golden hair, her shoulders sagged. “It’s not all on you. I bear responsibility for that as well.”

“You asked for trips and I always said we didn’t have money or couldn’t take time away from the farm.”

Things had gotten so bad, it was tough for him to see beyond the next chore. He kept thinking if he worked harder, he could fix the mess they were in. But all he’d done was dig them in deeper by sacrificing their marriage.

“And I didn’t push. I could have pressed, and you would have agreed. But to be honest, I let it slide because trips make me anxious. Because of what happened to my parents.”

Had he known that? Sometimes he forgot how much she’d faced on her own. Her life had been tough before him, and he’d wanted to make it easier. Better.

But he hated how he’d failed her.

His throat bobbed. He skimmed a careful hand down her back. Fingers soaking in the way she leaned, ever so slightly, into the first real embrace they’d had in months. Not an impulsive kiss, but a real connection. A knowing silence settled in the air.

She loosed a cloudy white breath into the cool

autumn air. "I'm sorry I let you and the kids down with that."

"Nina, honey, don't think for a minute you've let us down. That's just not true." He hadn't thought about how her parents' deaths might make her feel about vacations. She'd never talked about it much, just that they'd been on a boating trip and she'd been home. In talking about it with her, they'd focused more on the sadness of having lost their parents, not so much on how it happened. "We're here now."

And underneath the stars, the girls chowing down on hot dogs, heads keeping time with the lively tune, he saw a happy life. A happy family, as Nina stayed leaning into his back rub. Roiling regret rose in his chest.

If only it wasn't pretend. If only he could secure this moment, let it take root. Because he had to make it work, and he would do anything—whatever it took—to keep his family together.

Even if it meant participating in the next activity designed to haul his feelings up and out, no matter how painful.

Nina popped the last bite of her s'more in her mouth, careful to catch all the oozing marshmallow. Beneath bright fall stars and a crooked crescent moon, she felt brighter. Though that been true all day. Especially during goat yoga, which had her laughing until her sides hurt. She couldn't remember when she'd last let go like that with her husband, just leaned into his strength, absorbed it, relaxed for a moment and felt the security of his arms around her. How she'd missed that.

The lady leading the "pack-tivity" had said it was supposed to be an icebreaker, that they needed to learn when to relax and not take things too seriously. Of course that had been a bait and switch, since now they were supposed to write their regrets on a piece of paper and burn it in the fire.

She clutched the tiny pencil in her hand, still surprised at herself for letting her guard down with him earlier in the evening. She couldn't deny, though, that it felt good to admit that she'd played a role in the emotional distance between them. Maybe she should continue to let her guard down, get closer to Douglas and work to heal things enough that they could co-parent as a divorced couple. Her hand trembled holding the pencil.

What was Douglas writing? Did she really want to know or would it just make things harder?

Squinting for a moment, she glanced toward his cramped handwriting. All it would take was a simple look since he sat so close that his leg pressed against hers. She shook off the temptation to lean closer, to take a peek into his thoughts, and yes, just to *be* closer. Then, rising, he tossed his paper into the flames before striding away, and the moment was gone.

She turned her attention to her own scrap of paper. There felt like so many things to offer the fire. To release.

Some folks, like an older gentleman in a thick college sweatshirt, tossed their regrets into the fire without much fanfare, the crackling flame sending the slip of paper sailing to satisfy the hunger of the flame. Other Top Dog campers leaned more into verbal rituals. Spoke their regrets to the fire before sending the paper to join kindling.

And then there were those who looked as if they didn't have a care in the world. Auburn pigtails framed the freckled face of a woman in her early twenties, mud flecking the thigh of her jeans. She leaned against a tree, looking sidelong at a broad-chested young man with matching mud flecks on his jeans. Their name tags identified them as Top Dog stable staff. The young man had a piece of hay in his curly brown hair that the auburn woman, probably a local college student, pulled out and tapped him on the nose with.

A smile curved his lips as he snatched the hay strand from her before tucking it behind her ear, his hand lingering on her jawline. Even from here, she could see it—the spark, the promise of youth.

Had she and Douglas looked that young back when they'd met?

Pressing pen to paper, Nina made smooth, deliberate marks on the page. Each letter formed an incantation and realization. Underlining the phrase for emphasis, she allowed herself one moment to take in the weight of the page.

Scrawled in her neat cursive, she'd committed her regret to paper. Even more than the loss of her marriage, she regretted that her children would feel grief. A unique loss of their own. A death of sorts, even though both parents lived. Although she and Douglas would try to create a peace for them over time, there was still that pain to wade through. From the depths of her gut, her chest squeezing tight as she folded the paper. Line crisp. Private.

Rising from the pink-and-gold quilt beneath the tree where her family was gathered, Nina strode to the fire, her boot steps determined as leaves crunched beneath her. She tossed the scrap into the fire. Silently she watched the smoke rise and trail into the dark sky. Her eyes met her husband's as he stood on the other side of the fire. So tempting. It was one thing to be vulnerable with him.

It was another to let the attraction flame out of control.

Turning her back to the warm fire and his compelling stare, she returned to the quilt, settling next to Kacie. She leaned into her daughter and nudged her with a shoulder. "Your dad told me you've been up late practicing your roping."

"There's a big competition coming up." Her blue eyes gleamed with determination. "I'm going to win."

"Dedication and hard work are good things."

"Thanks. So why do you have that look in your eyes?"

Nina scooted back, leaning on her palms. The stretch loosened some of the sore muscles from the goat yoga poses earlier. "What look?"

"The one you get when you have a mom speech coming up."

She laughed in surprise. "I didn't realize I do that."

"It looks kinda like this." Kacie scrunched her face, brows knitting together. She pressed her palms to her scrunched face, exaggerating as a giggle twined with the sounds of the fiddle.

There was so much joy in this place, in this moment with all those regrets turned to ashes. "I used to say the same thing to my mother."

"You don't talk about her much." Kacie played with a stick, moving dirt around the perimeter of the wedding-ring quilt.

"I don't? I should be better about that. She was

a great mom and she deserves to be remembered and celebrated."

Shadows darkened Kacie's usually bright, attentive eyes, her jaw tightening in the same way Douglas's did when he was fighting back emotion. "I don't know what I'd do if I lost my parents."

"It's the hardest thing I have ever gone through."

"I'm sorry, Mom. I can see why you wouldn't want to talk about it."

"You do know the odds are low that anything would happen to me and your dad."

"But what if it happened anyway? You gotta admit, our luck hasn't been the best," she said, tentatively. She caught her breath before blurting out in a strained voice. "I don't have any grandparents. Uncle Tyler is dead. You don't have any brothers or sisters. I don't want to go to foster care."

"Oh, Kacie, I'm so very sorry you've had that on your heart. You don't have to worry." Nina brushed a thumb over her daughter's cheeks, holding her slender face. She worked a smile to her mouth. "You know the Jacksons, right?"

"They're the ones who got everyone together to help watch over the farm while we're here."

"Yes, they did. Well, they have agreed that if something—heaven forbid—were to happen to me and your dad, they would become your guardians. Trust me, I would not let what happened to me happen to you and Kelsey."

Kacie swallowed. Twice. "Thanks, Mom." She scrubbed her face, the weight falling from her as a wry smile tugged at the corners of her mouth. "Maybe the Jacksons would let us get a trampoline."

Nina elbowed her playfully. "Should I worry?"

Kacie's arms snaked around Nina's waist, squeezing hard, the hug all the more special as they became rarer the older her daughter grew. Then Kacie shot to her feet before bounding away.

Back pressed against the bark of an oak tree, Nina watched Douglas play tag with the girls a safe distance away from the blaze of the fire. Others joined in the timeless game. Out here, woods and mountains around them, she could imagine other families having done the same.

As she turned her attention to the flame, the activity of the day settled into her bones. The fire danced and her eyelids drooped after the day spent in the fresh air. Sleep tugged at her, along with the sense of comfort this place gave her, and she surrendered to the need to shut her eyes for just a moment…

Nina stomped around her bedroom flinging her suitcase on the carpeted floor. She wasn't allowed to go on the boating trip. And worse yet, Mrs.

Donovan, the widow from next door who smelled like talcum powder and mothballs, was staying with her for the weekend.

Being a teenager was hard. Her parents just didn't understand how frustrating it was that nobody listened to her. She just wanted some independence. She was thirteen, nearly fourteen. Not a kid anymore. Still, they kept treating her like one. Maybe if they'd had other children they wouldn't be so obsessed with her. Having some sisters, or even brothers, would be nice. Her parents said there wasn't enough money for more children.

Her folks always worried about money. They said that was why they wanted her to think about a practical career. That photography was a hobby.

She'd been so excited when they saved up to buy a used boat, planning all the photos she would take, maybe even one that she could have blown up and framed for her wall to hang alongside the Annie Leibovitz and Steve McCurry posters. She just wanted a little adventure, a simple boat ride.

Then the dream imagery shifted, changing too swiftly for her to get her bearings until she was suddenly standing on the shoreline. But it was also her room with a lake coming into view, Nina watching her parents cruise by on the boat. Smoke billowed from the engine as it smacked into an-

other vessel. She saw the panic on her parents' faces. Tried to scream...

And then she was on the boat. Her parents faded, replaced by Douglas and the girls. Water pouring over the sides, higher, as they sank...

Gasping, Nina sat up so fast her head knocked the tree trunk, bark rasping against her skull. Blinking fast, her eyes adjusted to the dark, campfire now nothing more than coals. She breathed deeper, drawing in gulps of air, the panic of drowning still clinging to her.

The music had stopped. People were standing and folding their blankets. Her husband was staring down at her, hand extended. Their daughters behind him, gathering up their backpacks.

This evening had been a beautiful time away, but she would do well to remember their purpose for coming to the Top Dog Dude Ranch. To help their children see that even though they were splitting, she and Douglas could still get along as parents. They would still be a family, just living in separate homes.

But she absolutely couldn't afford for them to harbor false hopes. She understood all too well how much it hurt to lose the perfect family.

Rope sailing toward the sheep, Kacie's breath caught in her chest. Waiting for the loop to deliver as she pictured it in her mind. The throw landed true. Satisfied, she released the hold.

Ready to start again.

It was the fifth time in a row the lasso had landed as she planned. She felt like she'd found her stride.

Murmurs and snippets of conversation grew louder. With a quick glance over her shoulder, she took in a gathering crowd of folks dressed warmly. Watching *her.*

She stood up straighter and added a little flair to her wrist movement as she swung the lasso again. Simple stuff really, but she enjoyed the way folks at the petting zoo oohed and ahhed like she was doing something special. This was certainly a lot more fun than Kelsey's dumb goat yoga. The baby goats were cute enough, but they climbed all over everyone at the worst possible times until people were a tangle of arms and legs.

The least the silly critters could have done was topple her parents into each other so maybe they would quit looking at each other like they wanted to kiss. So much for the power of magic animals. Her parents had spent most of the session laughing instead. Smiling, even.

It made her gut knot, seeing them look at each other like they used to, making her want something when she'd convinced herself it was better they just get things over with.

Could there be something to what Kelsey said about giving them another chance?

She sneaked a glance at her mom again, but her parents weren't standing close anymore. Her mom's head turned toward the grandmother, her daughter and granddaughter.

Cupping her hands around her mouth, the grandmother shouted, "You're on fire, lovely."

Her cheeks blazed with heat. So often, it was Kelsey who won all the praise from adults. She never had a grandma or a grandpa. The other kids at school would tell stories about spending the summer with their grandparents, or getting spoiled at Christmas. She was sad to miss out on that. But mostly sad her parents didn't have parents anymore.

Wind whipped through the grounds of the petting zoo. The scent of hay carried through as the breeze chilled all the skin on her hands and cheeks—everything not covered by her new green Top Dog Dude Ranch sweatshirt. A couple of kids stood in a pen, taking turns feeding a baby lamb with a bottle. Another little boy was putting coins in a machine spitting out pet treats like gumballs. Some kids were gathering eggs in the chicken coop like it wasn't a daily chore.

Though the brim of her father's Stetson shadowed his eyes, Kacie could tell that Dad was having an enthusiastic conversation with Jacob, the ranch owner who'd just arrived to the fence. Her dad didn't talk to many people these days, not since Uncle Tyler died.

Beyond the sheep, Kacie tracked the movement of a young couple feeding pigs. They held hands tight. How could she get her parents to do that?

Amplified by the wind, the ranch owner's voice carried over to Kacie as she set herself up to throw the lasso again. "When she's older, we should hire her to be a part of our summer camp. Or maybe you could even start your own program on your farm. She certainly is a natural."

"You should see her ride." He rocked back on his boot heels. "The girl has a gift."

Kacie made her eyes focus on the sheep in front of her. But still registered the movement of chickens pecking at the scattered seed by one of the stable hands—a girl with red hair.

"When we went riding, she certainly looked like she was born in the saddle," Jacob's answer rumbled back.

Her dad rubbed along the back of his neck like he always did when he was tense. "It's good to see her so confident and happy."

She let the lasso fly, trying to not get psyched out by all the compliments.

The grandmother chuckled. “I can’t imagine her any other way.”

“Since her sister jumped ahead in school, Kacie has struggled with insecurity.”

Her lips went tight and she flung her lasso hard. Missing. Ugh. Didn’t they know she could hear them? And even though she should just move away, she couldn’t stop eavesdropping.

“It’s hard enough not to be competitive with your siblings. I can’t imagine what it’s like for twins.”

No. Kidding.

Kelsey’s voice rang out from across the petting zoo. She played with the hem of her pale pink Top Dog Dude Ranch sweater. “Hey, Mom and Dad, come over and check out the llama.”

Her parents approached from their opposite corners, but stood on either side of their daughter. No surprise.

Still, there was no denying that her sister was 100 percent correct about the ranch being the right place to help their parents. And being here together, as a family? It made Kacie’s chest ache wanting it to be forever. It was scary to want something so much. But now that she’d stopped hiding from it, she needed to do something. To make something happen. No doubt, this was their last chance and time was ticking away on their days at the dude ranch.

Well, Kelsey thought she knew everything, planning and overplanning. Kacie knew that sometimes you had to shake things up, even if that meant taking the reins and tampering with the schedule.

Chapter Seven

Who would have thought when he'd teased his wife about getting a couples' massage that somehow a snafu in the schedule would land them on two tables, side by side in their cabin's great room? While this wouldn't have been his pick, he now wondered why he hadn't made it happen before. The view of his wife was incredible, and he was thoroughly enjoying looking his fill.

A hand's reach away, Nina lay on her stomach, a sheet draped over the sweet curve of her bottom, but she was otherwise bare. Her creamy shoulders glowed with oil. His only regret? That he wasn't the one stroking her back.

A husband-and-wife massage team—Patsy and Lonnie—had put them both at ease with stories about their grandchildren. They'd even brought their little Pomeranian named Waylon, the orange fluff ball currently curled up snoozing under Nina's table. The scent of lavender clung to the air, instrumental guitar music flowing through a portable speaker. Candles flickered along the fireplace mantel.

He hadn't wanted to push her the night of the bonfire when she'd let him hold her. It had been a good start, but he wanted to build on that. Granted, it would be a challenge to keep things platonic between them once this massage was done. He couldn't even keep his eyes off the graceful line of her arm draped over the side of the table. What he wouldn't give to kiss his way from her fingers, to the sensitive crook of her elbow, all the way to her shoulder. Then ease her onto her back and… He cut the thoughts short before he embarrassed himself with an erection in front of Patsy and Lonnie.

They were a chatty duo and had offered a couple of times to quiet down, but Nina encouraged them. And he had to admit, it made things less awkward as they rambled on about their grandchildren.

Lonnie kneaded along Douglas's neck and shoulders as they neared the end of their hour.

"One year at Christmastime, we took the grandkids to Dollywood. And Alexa got sick after riding the Lightning Rod. Her brother teased her about that for years. Even made a little song about it to taunt her when her friends came over."

Patsy laughed, sweeping aside a strand of Nina's blond hair that had fallen loose onto her arm, sticking to the shiny oil. "That reminds me about when we took them to Nashville. Remember how Alexa and Andre sang Johnny Cash songs with me as we drove to the Country Music Hall of Fame?"

Lonnie pumped the bottle attached to her waist, oil streaming into her palm, releasing a fresh whiff of lavender. "She's doing her best to instill a love of country music. Aren't you, Patsy?"

"Well, I was named for Patsy Cline, after all," she said, sidestepping her pup as little Waylon scampered to find a bone, then settled back down to sleep again. "Is the temperature on the table okay?"

"Perfect," Nina moaned in a way that made him want to moan for another reason entirely. "I bet this would have worked wonders for Douglas after a cold winter day in the saddle."

Patsy shifted to Nina's head, massaging her scalp. "Is this a second honeymoon for you two?"

Douglas held his breath waiting for her answer.

"Actually, we're here with our daughters," Nina

said, her voice flat, neutral. "They, uh, told us about the Top Dog Dude Ranch and here we are."

"Awww," Patsy crooned. "How sweet that you're still making time for each other while the kids are off doing their own thing. Tending the husband-and-wife relationship is just as important as being parents."

Lonnie chuckled, massaging small circles along Douglas's jaw. "If the mama and daddy are happy, the kids are happy."

Great. So much for relaxing.

Nina let loose a sleepy laugh, though, surprising him. She cranked one eye open to peer at him. "Remember our honeymoon?"

"When we went white-water rafting and you got seasick?" he said instead.

"I sure do." Her muffled voice drifted through the face cradle. "Pregnancy hormones in overdrive."

He'd loved her so much but had also been scared to death about impending fatherhood. What did he know about being a dad? His dad had been a workaholic who barely spoke to his kids. Even at dinner, when he wanted something, he would thump his fist on the table, then point to what he wanted.

Douglas pulled his thoughts from the past before it tensed his muscles all back up again. "We spent the rest of the honeymoon by the fire..."

"Eating a romantic dinner of crackers, crackers and more crackers."

Regret pinched him. "I wish I had taken you on a real honeymoon."

She reached to touch his arm lightly, setting his skin on fire. "You tried. Three times as I recall."

He'd booked a weekend at a cabin for a snowy retreat, then the twins got ear infections.

Next time, he'd tried for a totally different vibe and booked a beach condo. A hurricane hit.

Thinking that surely the third time would be a charm, in a year that money had actually been plentiful for once, he'd booked a cruise. Tyler's accident happened the day before they were supposed to leave. At least they hadn't left already with the girls there alone.

Life had been about day-to-day survival after that.

"Mr. Archer," Lonnie's baritone cut through his thoughts. "You need to relax. Take a deep breath. Now let it out slowly. Is this your first massage?"

Nina looked over at him, her blond hair piled high on her head in a beautiful—tempting—tumble. "His first massage and our first couples' massage. But he gave me a spa certificate for Mother's Day one year."

"Ah, good man." Lonnie pressed Douglas's

temples, nearing the end of the massage. "But why not treat yourself, too, sir?"

There hadn't been time, really; he'd always wanted to make sure everyone else was taken care of.

Nina adjusted the sheet more securely. "He's not much for pampering."

Actually, what he'd said was that pampering made him feel weak. His brother had torn him up for the comment, reminding him of all the massages Tyler had gotten as a baseball player.

Which then also reminded Douglas of all his brother had given up to stay on the farm for him. He cleared his throat. "I'm learning to appreciate the experience."

And he really appreciated the view of his wife's bare skin, a view he didn't get to enjoy these days.

Patsy chuckled softly.

Lonnie backed away from the table. "Well, Mr. and Mrs. Archer, that concludes our session for today. Feel free to take your time getting up. We will collect our tables when you are at dinner."

Douglas's gaze locked with his wife's. The room echoed with the sounds of the couple packing their bags, silencing the music, then the door quietly clicking after them. Leaving him alone. With his beautiful wife. Romantic music playing in the background, candles flickering on the mantel.

She gazed back at him, her brown eyes darkening with pupils widening, aroused. Tendrils of fire passed between them. Nina's delicate arm was outstretched in the space between them, hanging off the side of the table.

Without sitting up, he reached toward her. She didn't pull away or say a word. So he took that as encouragement and stroked a finger down her hand. She started breathing faster, her lips parting.

The feel of her silky skin, even those few inches, tempted him more than he could remember. It had been so long since they'd caressed each other. Line dancing and the half kiss didn't count. Not like this, such an intimate moment for its understated nature.

Then her hand curled into a fist and the moment was lost. Regret burned through him, and even as he told himself to be patient, he was tired of waiting for his life to return to some semblance of normalcy.

Scrambling for something to say to either recapture the moment or diffuse the too-awkward tension between them, he swung his legs off the side, the sheet gathering around his waist.

A noise from under the table nearly startled him into dropping his sheet. Paws click, click, clicking on the ground had Douglas snapping to attention, pulling him from the moment of broken potential. Little Waylon—apparently forgotten by his owners—darted out in a flurry of orange fur.

Nina squealed. The Pomeranian looked back, took a corner of her sheet in his mouth. Then yanked, the linen tumbling off the table like a waterfall.

With his wife wearing nothing but blue lace panties.

While being naked in front of her husband wasn't anything new, Nina felt the heat of a blush cover her from head to toe. So much so, she barely felt the whoosh of cold air as the fluffy pooch ran around the room with the sheet fluttering behind them like a parachute.

Hand over her chest, she grasped to catch the sheet, so close. Her fingertips brushed the very edge. Her hand curled, almost plucking.

Douglas gave chase in nothing but his boxer briefs, calling out to the mischievous canine. "Come. I mean it. Come right now."

The elusive cotton slipped away as the pup ran under the sofa.

So much for modesty. She stood by the cabin's fireplace, bare except for her blue lace panties.

Dim lighting from the chandelier streamed

down on him, broad shoulders still glistening from the oils. Her heart stuttered. Her breath caught. And oh my, how she craved.

Frozen in place, the heat of his gaze making her flesh tingle, she wanted to say something, anything, but her mouth went dry. Her mind went blank. Her libido was shouting so loud it overshadowed anything else.

Quietly, he passed his sheet to her, arm extended.

She would have thought him unaffected, but his chest rose and fell faster, his pulse throbbing in his neck, his erection straining against his boxers.

Reaching, she took the sheet from his grasp, their fingers skimming each other. The crackle in the air was so much more than static. It was a current connecting them in the way it always had. On this level, at least, they'd always been compatible.

And then she was in his arms, the dog all but forgotten, her naked chest against his. She couldn't help but soak in the beautifully familiar sensation of him, the heat of his skin against hers.

His mouth against hers.

He stroked along her back, trailing up and down her spine.

Pressing closer and yet nowhere near enough, she swept her tongue against his, warm and spicy. She'd missed him, missed this. She loved kissing and her husband sure knew how to kiss, pouring everything into the moment in the way that could only draw her in. Lure her. In this, at least, he didn't hold back or put up walls. He was alive with emotion, heat, all the tumult he hid from the world.

Without breaking the connection, he backed her toward the leather sofa, the massive couch just the right size for the two of them. He reclined her back into the butter-soft leather, the lavender scent of the massage oil heavy in the air between them.

The fire in the hearth crackled and sparked like an echo to the flames between them. She hitched her leg up, stroking her foot along the back of his calf. The weight of him anchored her to the sofa, to the moment.

He skimmed kisses along her jaw, her neck, while palming her breast. She arched into his touch, a husky moan slipping from between her lips. "I've missed you."

His growl vibrated against her flesh. "I've missed you, too, woman, every day." He nuzzled her ear. "Let's move this to the other room so you can get your diaphragm."

Her blood iced in her veins. "I left it at home. I didn't think, expect, that we would..."

"Right," he said, his voice clipped as he shifted off her to sit. He scrubbed a hand through dark hair still tousled from her frantic fingers. "And I don't have condoms."

Her body screamed a great big no as the moment slipped further out of reach. "It's a safe time of the month. You know I'm so regular there's no guesswork—"

He shot to his feet, holding a hand up as if to put even another barrier between them. "How can you even think about risking a pregnancy? Our marriage is on the rocks. We are about to lose our home."

Tugging the sheet from under the couch, she wrapped the length around her body as he pulled on his jeans. The little Pomeranian scampered out, exploring the room. She had bigger worries right now than chasing the pup. "I understand that, trust me, I do. That's why I've fought so hard to hold on to the place. But Douglas, it's just that. A place."

"You couldn't be more wrong about that. Maybe it's because you grew up moving around so much. But losing the farm is losing a piece of myself I can never get back."

Pulse thudding, Nina turned his dismissal of her opinion over in her head, made all the worse by him so casually noting her chaotic childhood.

True, they were in financial trouble and she didn't want to lose the only real home she'd ever known. But she also knew what it was like to thrive in new places. His rebuke about home being land-specific instead of people-oriented had her reeling.

Breathing deeply, she struggled to rein in her temper and keep her voice steady, calm. "Douglas, you don't cease to exist as a person the day the land passes to someone else."

"And that's where you're wrong. That land is as much a part of my family as any person. It's been the core of our family for over a hundred years." He shook his head, looked down and away, snatched up the fire poker and jabbed at the logs. "I don't expect you to understand."

"Because I didn't grow up with roots? That's very condescending of you, don't you think?"

He stayed silent, shifting his gaze to the Pom pup as he curled up on top of the sheet on the floor.

Simmering heat sped through Nina's veins. Soft cloth still clinging to her skin, she stood straighter. "Then do like I suggested the last time we fought and don't give up on the farm."

"That's only delaying the inevitable—filing for bankruptcy. At least this way, we'll have our credit intact and maybe enough left over to buy the girls a pizza."

Last time they'd fought about this, she'd begged him to think outside the box. Even if their marriage was on the rocks, at least he would have his family's land; the girls would have that connection.

He brushed off the suggestion, dismissing her plea for creativity as a pie-in-the-sky fantasy. Numbers—reason—didn't lie.

That had been such a splash of cold water, that he didn't respect her as a person. He didn't see the value of what she brought to the relationship.

Marriages rarely died from one event. She'd learned the hard way that the collapse too often came one nail at a time. Somehow, she'd allowed herself to be so enchanted by this place that she'd lost sight of that and started to think of them as a couple.

From now on, no more couples' events. They were here for the girls, as a family. Every choice would include both of their pint-sized chaperones. Because one thing was certain.

The last thing she and Douglas needed was an accidental pregnancy.

Rain hammered the roof of the ice cream parlor as Douglas cranked the ice cream churn, the day full of storms having canceled out their scheduled canoeing trip and bird watching. They'd substituted their sensory day with indoor activities—soap making and ice cream churning.

An array of small cups with pastel-colored

spoons were arranged in a perfect circle—probably Kelsey's doing—at the center of the table where Nina and the girls sat. Kacie snatched one of the little sample sizes from in front of her sister, a whooping laugh of joy as she tried the small container with the pastel green spoon.

Nina's focus stayed with the table, avoiding his gaze. He and Nina hadn't spent more than five minutes alone since their couples' massage debacle. Even at night, she made a point of being in bed before him, her back to him and utterly silent by the time he parked himself on the futon. And once he woke up, she had their agenda planned out to the second.

Now they were the proud bearers of a bag of goat's milk soap bars, scented with lavender, citrus, jasmine. All for stress relief.

Which moved them along to the bakery/ice cream parlor. Apparently, this was Mrs. O'Brien's domain. Bone Appétit was a small, brightly lit parlor. Four tables of guests were arranged on the brown-tiled floor, surrounded by walls brimming with chocolates and baked goods. Warm yellow lights made the space cozier, homey. Really homey to him in particular. Bone Appétit had its guests work together to churn ice. He was surprised the girls had chosen this activity since it was a common occurrence for them growing up on a dairy farm.

Scents of cinnamon and vanilla clung to the space filled with wrought iron tables and chairs on the patio as well as inside. There were two sides to the shop, one with human treats and one with pooch treats. Ice cream. Cakes. Cookies.

The dogs around here got treats too—pup-sicles and pup-cakes. Off to the left at the tiniest table sat a couple in their thirties fawning all over each other like newlyweds. A beagle lay at the husband's feet and the wife placed a pup-cake shaped like a paw in front of the dog. The beagle lifted his head and let loose a bay of approval.

Douglas had to confess, the O'Briens had their act together when it came to planning events with a dual purpose. It wasn't just about enjoyment. All the sessions were firmly rooted in farming, while keeping in focus the benefits of living a back-to-nature lifestyle. Somehow he'd lost sight of those advantages, focusing only on the stressors.

And now it was too late for him to tune in to those things on his family's homestead.

He cleared his throat, scrubbing a hand over his face. "I'm sorry about my lack of self-control. The last thing I want is to upset you. To hurt you."

"You have nothing to apologize for. We're both adults and we've certainly said worse to each other." Nina spooned up a sample of the mint chocolate chip ice cream. The tightness on her face eased with a blissful sigh as she savored the taste.

He wished she still sighed like that for him. "That doesn't make it right."

Her bright eyes pierced right through him. "Today, we can just chalk it up to sexual frustration."

Well, that was certainly true enough. He was on sensory overload. The scents of the soaps made him imagine rubbing the bars over his wife's body. The lemony taste of ice cream had him fantasizing about sharing the spoon after sex. All thoughts that were making him increasingly uncomfortable.

He searched for something benign to say. Small talk had never been his forte. "Which flavor's your favorite?"

"The buttercream is amazing. I thought I'd tasted the best of the best back home, but Hollie has quite a talent with her recipes. I can only imagine what it would taste like with fresh milk from our cows."

Kacie and Kelsey shot to their feet, excitement animating their steps as they picked their way over to the sampling station. Despite their physical appearance, the girls were different sides of a coin. Wearing light jeans, boots and a flannel shirt, Kacie leaned on the counter decorated with fall leaves and mini hay bales. Kelsey stood straight next to her sister, waiting with patience as Hollie bustled behind the counter even as she fidgeted with her fuzzy daisy-and-sunflower pullover. So reserved and careful it tugged at a parent's heart.

He drank in the sight. Had it really been years since they were little more than a pound each fighting for their lives in incubators? "They've grown up so fast. I know every parent says that, but I just didn't know until I lived it."

"We have plenty to be grateful for." She toyed with the neckline of her sweater. "There were so many days I wasn't sure even one of them would live, much less both of them."

"Remember when we celebrated them graduating from a feeding tube to a bottle?" Even thinking about that day made him choke up, even a decade later. Those first weeks of their life had been filled with unrelenting fear, so strong even the memory of it squeezed the air from his lungs. Thank God, those days had passed and he would never have to return to that nightmare.

"Kelsey first, while our stubborn Kacie held out a while longer." She smiled, her eyes sheened with tears.

"I worry sometimes that Kacie's struggles in school trace back to those early days." He scrubbed at the back of his neck.

She touched his knee lightly. "I didn't know you worried about that. But if it's an issue, we'll do whatever we need to help her."

Her touch seared through denim.

He cleared his throat. "I try to tell myself she's happy excelling in her own interests, but it's clear she's hurt by Kelsey's academic success."

"Life isn't fair or evenhanded."

He nodded, his mind jumping to the past. "I see them in my sleep, so tiny with all those tubes running from their frail preemie bodies."

A lump formed in his throat, remembering the sterile scent of the hospital. The panic that only came from knowing something was out of your hands. How could she even think of risking that again with another pregnancy?

Lines of panic drew Nina's lips tighter. "I never thought it would be my only experience with childhood. I always imagined we would make happy, normal memories of leaving the hospital with our healthy seven-pound newborn—"

She stopped short, looking at him in panic and blinking fast against the sheen in her eyes.

He'd never considered how his decision to not to have more children could have had deeper repercussions for her. He'd stolen yet another dream from her without even knowing it. He'd been so focused on how their shared grief then had been—and still was—so powerful, so gut-wrenching.

If he could just make her understand where he was coming from, if he could just find the right words. Douglas cupped her shoulder, squeezing lightly. “Nina, I can see that you’re upset and that’s the—”

She shrugged off his hand, her body going tense in that way he knew meant she was struggling to hold on to control. Wrought iron scraping against the floor, she stood up from her seat in a start. “I, uh, need to talk to Hollie about what pastries the girls would like with their ice cream.”

As if the girls hadn’t been choosing their own food since they could point.

Watching his wife’s blond hair gather on her sweater as she made her way toward the countertop, he couldn’t dodge the uncomfortable truth that saying no to another baby had nothing to do with money, and everything to do with protecting his heart from any more loss.

Chapter Eight

Nina struggled to resist Douglas on a regular day. But seeing her husband go all vulnerable and emotional over memories of their daughters?

That threatened to steal every bit of her resolve at a time she was more than a little raw from revisiting those early days when they didn't know if Kacie and Kelsey would survive. Douglas had been such a rock for her then, somehow she'd missed how the experience had gutted him, too.

Lordy, he was a complex man, and he had a way of getting to her even when they were surrounded by a roomful of people in the Bone Appétit Café. Standing at Hollie's shop counter,

Nina placed bite-size apple tarts onto the white-and-gold polka-dot serving tray. She breathed in vanilla, a scent she always associated with the holidays and laughter.

If only she could bottle up that mood and dispense accordingly. Nina could see Hollie's stamp all over the place, from the white picket fence sectioning off a play area to the mural of dogs romping through the mountains painted on the walls. She had to admire the way Hollie O'Brien had managed to blend her culinary background with her husband's animal husbandry training. Nina had never quite managed that balancing act. She'd been so intent on helping Douglas keep his family dream alive, she'd lost sight of her own.

Being here, with the world slowing down and her senses coming back to life, the artist inside her was ravenous to be fed after so long in hibernation. She ached to capture every vibrant image around her. Why did she have to tamp down all the parts of herself that Douglas had once claimed were what made him fall for her?

Hollie leaned into Nina's line of sight. An easy smile played on her lips as she wiped her hand on her burlap apron covered in ice cream cones with pawprint-shaped ice cream. "Your husband appears to be a really good father."

Because he was.

Nina handed over plates for pie. "You and Jacob make a cute couple. I admire how you make it seem so easy to work together."

Hollie poured heavy cream into an aluminum bowl. Then dumped a heap of powdered sugar before adding a splash of vanilla. "Marriages are complicated. Business is easy."

Nina sighed as images of the Archer farm danced through her mind's eye. The first real home she'd ever had. Even when her parents were alive, they'd moved all the time. "Successful businesses are."

"Well, I guess that helps." Hollie set to stirring the mixture, metal beater clinking against the bowl as whipped cream for the pie began to form. "We've been looking at land to expand, but sometimes I worry that if we take on more, we won't have any time for each other."

"How long have you been married?" Her gaze gravitated to Douglas, who was patiently herding the girls as they chose toppings to add to the ice cream.

"We've been together for over two decades." She leaned back against the counter, her eyes taking on a faraway look. "I was only sixteen when he walked into my daddy's ice cream parlor. He placed his order and asked me out all in one breath."

"That's fast."

"Oh, I said no." Hollie winked. "And continued to say no when he came to the shop faithfully once a week to repeat the invitation."

"How long did you hold out?"

"Four months and three weeks." Hollie grabbed an extra spoon and swiped a bit of the whipped cream, offering a sample to Nina.

"That's sure a long time. He never gave up?" Nina licked the spoon—and oh my God, that was the most divine whipped cream ever. Her taste buds cried out in bliss.

"Nope. He wasn't pushy, either. Just charmingly persistent." She toyed with the end of her braid. "Each week he would tell me a little something about himself and ask me something about myself. But it wasn't the things he told me that won me over. It was seeing the way he treated other people when he thought I wasn't looking."

Nina couldn't help but smile.

Hollie spooned dollops of cream on top of the slices of pie. "Like holding the door open for a gentleman with a cane. Tipping big to the waitress who needed it the most. Picking up a teddy bear off the floor to pass to an overwhelmed mom, and then shaking it to entertain the kid while the mother finished her milkshake in peace."

"He sounds like a good man." And she knew

from stories from the kids in her foster home that good people weren't just a given in life.

Hollie's face lit with a faraway look full of the first blush of love. "I can still remember what he bought on that very first day—a double scoop of chocolate in a waffle cone. He's always had a sweet tooth."

"How romantic that now you have your own ice cream parlor." A job she clearly loved.

"Well, it wasn't totally smooth sailing. He questioned my sanity when I said half the clientele would be animals."

"Smart business having the clients buy food to feed the ranch animals."

"The animals certainly gave the plan their blessing. They all gather round on pumpkin pup ice cream day." She swept off her apron and replaced it with a clean one. "So how did you and your man meet?"

Her man? Was he? Not for much longer.

"I was in college studying photography." So excited to be building a future for herself, determined never again to be dependent on anyone for anything. "During my wildlife photography class, we made a trip out to a local farm. They'd agreed to give us a tour of the spread and in return we would share our pictures with them. Day one, he led the tour, and I was hooked on photographing the outdoors. I knew exactly what I wanted to do with my life."

"You've been so generous in sharing your talent taking photos the past few days. I'd love to see some photos from your portfolio."

"Thanks, but it's woefully outdated. Kids. Life. Not that I regret them in any way. They are my most amazing accomplishment."

Hollie's eyebrows pinched together as she glanced at the kids, a smile flickering across her face, if not her eyes. "They're certainly two of the most enthusiastic young guests we've ever had. What's on your agenda for this evening?"

"The girls chose the drive-in movie."

Hollie elbowed her lightly. "With luck, your daughters will drift off to sleep so you and your husband are free to make out."

Nina's eyes went wide and her stomach fell to her feet. It was just a drive-in, she reassured herself. Nothing had to happen. She could always say no.

So why was she already trying to figure out the best place to buy condoms?

Sitting in the back of his truck under the stars, Douglas stretched his legs on the quilt, his wife beside him for movie night. And what a shame there would be no necking. After their argument about birth control, it was clear he had more work to do in charming her before taking her to bed.

So he tamped down the need throbbing through his veins and focused on the moment, glad to be outside now that the rain had passed. A family-friendly movie about a dog's trek to reunite with her owner was splashed across the makeshift screen—the side of a mountain with stone chiseled flat. Their daughters sat on the tailgate, legs swinging as they finished off the last of their popcorn.

The movie was entertaining, but he would much rather keep his eyes on his wife. Her hair was loose tonight, lifting ever so slightly in the wind. She made even jeans and a sweatshirt look like runway fashion with her knee-high leather boots and big gold hoop earrings. She was even more beautiful than the day they'd met.

They had traveled a lot of heartache since then.

Kacie held up her empty popcorn bucket. "Hey, can Kelsey and I get more snacks?"

Kelsey shifted onto her knees to face them. "Please? The stand is just over there." She pointed to the flatbed trailer behind a tractor to the left of the movie "screen."

"They've got hot cocoa with marshmallows," Kacie added, "and those big fat pretzels with cheese."

Nodding, Nina untangled a strand of hair from her earring. “Sure, just be sure to stay where we can see you.”

Their cheers echoing after them, they hopped off the back of the truck and darted past the van beside them, waving to the injured firefighter before sprinting off.

Douglas braced a hand on the truck bed, his palm flat just behind her, close enough that his arm was almost around her, but not so much to spook her. “The return of drive-in movies—at least something good came out of the pandemic.”

She tipped her face toward him, her long lashes sweeping upward, the moonlight sparkling in her eyes. “This place certainly has a way of making the most of the simple pleasures in life. A real back-to-basics approach.”

“They’re innovative, that’s for sure. My hat’s off to them for figuring out a way for their business to survive in a world that’s changing so much, so fast.” He wished he’d been able to do the same.

“Thank you for hanging in there with the soap making earlier.”

“It was important to you, which made it important to me.”

“I could tell it made you uncomfortable, talking about feelings with a bunch of strangers.”

The rose scent that the couple beside them had

chosen for their soap reminded him of his mother. Before he knew it, he was talking to the whole group about the sound of her voice as she sang him to sleep, something he hadn't even remembered until then.

"I wish I could blame it on being a guy, but I'm afraid it's much deeper in my DNA. Tyler, on the other hand, was always able to label whatever he was feeling." His brother could have led the whole soap-making class, spilling heart-tugging secrets left and right.

"Yes, he had a gift for that. Somehow that made it easier to process whatever emotions I was dealing with. I wasn't the only one in the room weighted down by something. I wasn't alone."

He hated that he hadn't been enough for her. That in many ways he still wasn't. "Tyler was there for me."

"And you were there for him."

"There to see him die." The words tasted bitter on his tongue.

"You know you did more than that." She touched a hand to his leg lightly, her gentle hand warm through well-worn denim. "You made it possible for him to live out the last days of his life on the farm he loved."

"With you and the girls there to make him smile." His world would be so very barren without them. “I’m sorry you had to sacrifice so much for me.”

“Douglas,” she said softly, sliding her hand away. “We’re going to have to talk to the kids soon.”

“I know.”

From lowered lashes, awash in movie glow and starlight, she looked at him, a gaze that pierced to his core. “Do you? I feel like you’re delaying because it’s going to be hard.” Compassion shone from her eyes, no sign of judgment, nothing to spur a fight that would have given him an excuse to walk away.

He had no choice but to answer her or distract her. “Or maybe I don’t think we should have the conversation at all.”

Forget about keeping his distance.

He sealed his mouth to hers.

Douglas tasted like popcorn and lost dreams. Passion and broken promises.

He tasted like her husband.

So much so, it made it hard to acknowledge the embers of anger that crackled inside her over his incendiary comment about forgoing a conversation with the girls about divorcing. As if she wanted to have the talk? She hated that they’d come to this. Grieved over all they’d lost.

And after having given up so many dreams,

she deserved this simple kiss, one that couldn't go anywhere since they weren't alone out here under the stars at the makeshift drive-in. Kissing. One of the married kinds of kisses that were their right to indulge in as a couple. Whatever he had to offer and everything she had to give. This wasn't a time for thinking. Just feeling. Experiencing. Reveling in the warmth pulsing through her.

She'd missed him, missed what they shared. Their desire for each other had never been in question. She didn't want to consider what it would be like to live without him, without this. Or how she would resist him at all the million times their paths would cross in the future.

Or what it would be like to see him with another woman someday.

The thought iced her, freezing out desire. She pulled back, palms pressing against his strong, chiseled chest. The feel of his muscles threated to draw her into the moment again. But she kept her resolve strong and inched across the truck bed. "I should go check to see what's keeping the girls."

He stared at her for moment, his eyes assessing, before he stopped her with a hand on her arm. "No need. I'll go."

She didn't bother arguing. As long as she got her space. "Fine. Thank you."

Dragging in a ragged breath, she fought to keep

her face neutral. Memories and feelings had been loosed by the press of his lips. Promises of what life could be if there had been another path.

He didn't even glance back as he jumped from the vehicle, his boots puffing dust as he landed. He made fast tracks past the firefighter couple on his way toward the girls, their blond ponytails just visible in the crowd around the refreshments area.

Restless, she inched forward to sit on the tailgate, watching him stride away, long legs eating up the distance between him and their daughters. Lord have mercy, he had a fine butt, just the right kind to fill out his jeans and make her hands ache to tuck inside his back pockets.

A cleared throat drew her attention back. Jolting, she searched…and found the injured firefighter staring up at her from where he sat on his blanket, his wheelchair beside him. His companion nowhere in sight. "How are you and your family enjoying your stay?"

She slid off the tailgate and leaned against the bumper. Dried leaves and the sweet scent of chocolate carried on a breeze that brought goose bumps to her skin, a phantom touch making her long for Douglas. "The place certainly lives up to its reputation. Are you and your wife having a good time?"

He shook his head. "She's actually my fiancée."

"Oh, well, congratulations."

"Thanks, but not for much longer." He reached for his water bottle, only to come up short. A curse hissed low. "Could you pass me that, please?"

"Of course." She scooped up the metal cylinder with a fire department logo blazoned on the side. "Here you go."

"Thanks. I hate asking, but such is life."

Remembering how Tyler hated for people to loom over him, she sat on the ground, cross-legged so that they were eye-to-eye. "It's no trouble, truly. Is there something else I can get for you?"

"A new life?" He shook his head fast. "Forget I said that. I came here hoping to find a way to finally make her understand we're over. Maybe you can help me with that."

Shadows cast by the movie screen lights danced over the man's hard jaw. His green eyes fixed on her as the weight of his question pressed on her. Her own experience with loss threatened to swallow her answer and still her tongue.

Pausing for a moment, she gathered her thoughts as she played with the hem of her sweatshirt. Material soft against her fingertips anchored her to an answer as she reflected back on the interactions between the man and his fiancée these past few days.

"I'm so sorry." She understood how much losing someone you loved hurt. “For what my opinion is worth, she doesn’t look at you like a woman who wants to go.”

“She’s stubborn, though, and honorable. She’s not going to leave me as long as I’m in the chair.” For a moment, the hard set of his jaw softened.

“What if you’re wrong?” She cut herself off short, heat flooding her cheeks. “It’s not my place to have said that. I’m sorry.”

“No need to apologize. I should be the one to apologize for dumping personal garbage on a complete stranger.”

Bursts of laughter erupted from the folks in the pickup to their left. Nina glanced to the screen, catching a snippet of a scene where the border collie character quirked her head at a frisky feline.

“This place has a way of breaking down barriers fast.” She scrunched her toes in her boots, cracking away the tension that had Douglas’s name stamped all over it.

“True enough. What brings you and your family here?”

“Our girls wanted a family vacation.” She paused. It would take a lot more Top Dog magic to get her comfortable enough to air her family’s dirty laundry. “Things have been stressful at home. We all need some peace.”

The man nodded as the on-screen dog barked—

which elicited a chorus of howls and baying from the dogs in the audience. "We broke up, then I went to work and had an accident during a call. She blames herself."

Nina swallowed, knowing all too well what carrying the aftermath of an accident did to a person. Wind stirred her hair, bringing the murmur of children squealing at the sight of the border collie helping the tabby cat across the river. "I can see where that would make things complicated."

And as the words left her mouth, she realized that she needed to take her own advice. If she wanted to indulge in one last moment to be with Douglas without risking hurting the girls, she needed to find a way for them to have space to talk, to be together, without interference.

And to do that? She needed to call in the cavalry.

"Will you excuse me for a moment? I need to make a phone call." Standing, she tugged her cell phone from her pocket and scrolled through her contacts until landing on the person she trusted most in the world.

Her foster sister Ashlynn.

Kelsey raised up onto her toes, looking for her sister, who'd ditched her while she was waiting in line. Her stomach knotted and her head throbbed.

If they didn't stick together, their parents would be mad. They would fight. Everything, all the hard work in getting the family here, would be ruined.

Swallowing down the need to be sick, she pushed through the crowd. "Kacie? Kacie, where are you? Kacie?"

Her head hammered harder. Was this what Uncle Tyler had felt like right before he had his aneurysm? Scared? Heart pounding?

Panicked?

And then she heard her sister's laugh. Thank goodness. Her stomach settled and the pressure in her temples eased. She followed the sound, dodging and weaving past people, sidestepping a pair of dachshunds on leashes just before they could tangle up her feet.

Finally, she caught a glimpse of her sister's blue hoodie. Hands shoved in her pockets, Kacie talked to a few boys standing in a circle. The tallest boy, maybe a year older than them, laughed as Kacie gestured wildly.

Kelsey narrowed her eyes, steps growing more determined as she broke into the circle to stand in front of her twin. She felt the eyes of the other kids press into her back.

Yanking on her twin's arm, Kelsey said with as much force as she could muster while still whispering, "Come on. Mom and Dad are waiting for their snacks."

"They don't even know we're gone." Kacie tugged her arm away. "The whole point of this trip is for them to have time together, so that's what I'm doing."

"We're not supposed to talk to strangers," she whispered through tight teeth.

Kacie rolled her eyes. "There are plenty of people here and staff, too, so we're safe. You're such a rule-follower."

"I may be a rule-follower, but you're a total slacker. Just look at your grades. You could get better marks if you tried."

Kacie shrugged her shoulders. "I don't care about school."

"You don't care about anything except playing with the horses and your lasso."

"Shows what you know. I'm not playing," she said with fire spitting from her eyes. "I'm gonna be a farmer like Dad and Uncle Tyler. Even like our grandpa. Like Dad always says, 'It's in our blood.' Not that I expect you to understand."

Kelsey swallowed down a huge lump in her throat. "Why do you hate me so much?"

Kacie's eyes went wide. "I don't hate you. You're my sister."

"I'm not just your sister. I'm your twin." Then shook her head. "Never mind. Forget it."

She pushed past her twin, anger and sadness at the distance everywhere in her family brewing, threatening to be released into a flurry of tears.

"Wait," Kacie called out after her. "I'm sorry. I don't know why I say things sometimes. My temper just gets in the way. You're my sister. Of course I love you."

Kacie tugged on her arm. Hard. Kelsey stopped walking, the leaves quieting beneath her feet. Her twin wrapped her in a tight hug.

"Then let's start working together, like we did with the dog washing. Look what we made happen." She needed to get Kacie on board with the right way to help their parents in case something happened to her.

"All right, brainiac, what do you have in mind?"

"Never mind." Kelsey started to spin away.

Sighing, Kacie grabbed her arm. "I'm sorry. Really. I was just teasing."

Jerking free, Kelsey fought back tears and kept on walking, because if she got teased over crying, she would lose it. Totally.

"Come on, Kelsey," Kacie pleaded, jumping in front of her. "How about this time I come up with an idea to make them work together?"

Now that caught her attention. "Like how?"

A slow smile spread over her sister's face. A kind of wicked smile.

This was going to be good. Because when Kacie set her mind to something, there was no stopping her.

Kacie hooked arms with her. "So, you know those kids I was talking to when you found me?"

Douglas stomped through the crowd of people who were carrying enough snacks for an army. The scent of popcorn and cheese nachos filled the air. Laughter mixed with the echoes of the movie speakers. Lights flickered as the projection against the mountain screen refracted back.

But there was no sign of his daughters. He knew the place had top-notch security—he'd checked before attending—but still. They were in the middle of the mountains with wild animals in the woods. He scanned the perimeter of the forest, far enough away that it was unlikely the girls could have gone there alone without being noticed.

Still.

He considered going back to check in with Nina, but he wanted to check behind the snack station. He'd been a fool to let himself get so distracted by his wife and her surprisingly enthusiastic response to that sizzling kiss. His own emotions were too close to the surface, courtesy of Top Dog prodding. Did every activity have to be about getting in touch with their feelings? This place was an exercise in torture designed to showcase his emotional shortcomings at every turn.

He was angry at the girls for wandering off, but even more upset with himself for not watching them more closely. He angled past a couple with a toddler on the dad's shoulders and searched for someone who might be able to help.

A father of three herded his children back toward an SUV with the trunk popped open. Pretzels and churros cradled in his arms, he chased after his children, all under ten.

Clusters of folks Douglas hadn't met formed a thick crowd by the hot cider and doughnut station. The sound of the cash register's antique bell mingled with the mounting movie music.

Jacob O'Brien leaned against a bale of hay, talking to the grandmother visiting the Top Dog Dude Ranch with her daughter and granddaughter. Her daughter and granddaughter huddled together a few feet in front of them, sitting on an orange-and-red quilt on the ground. A blanket was wrapped tight around them as the granddaughter bit into an oversize s'more.

Douglas charged forward, carefully picking his way around the quilt. "Excuse me, Jacob, sorry to interrupt."

Jacob pivoted toward him. “No problem at all. We were just shooting the breeze. Any chance you chased me down to talk about a land deal?”

“Actually, I’m just looking for my daughters. They went to pick up more snacks and haven’t returned. Have you seen them?”

“As a matter of fact, I sure have. They’re right over there.”

Douglas followed the direction of Jacob’s gesture toward a cluster of kids about the twins’ height. Kelsey was watching from the outskirts. And Kacie… A deeper look, and he located her in the center of the group…

Talking to—no, wait—*flirting* with a boy.

Chapter Nine

Perched on the tailgate of the truck, Nina held her cell phone to her ear. Once she'd decided to call Ashlynn for help, Nina hadn't wanted to wait a minute longer. Hopefully, her sister could come to the ranch. It was closer to Ashlynn and would save drive time, not to mention she was impatient.

But if not? Nina would be grateful for whatever her sister could do, even if only to offer a shoulder to cry on. Her sister picked up a moment later and Nina felt a rush of relief. "I'm so glad you're home. I was worried you'd be working."

"I'm actually on a quick break before closing," Ashlynn said. "How is the ranch? Is it everything the website promises? What are the girls doing? I want the lowdown."

"The place is everything they advertised and more. I can understand why they want to expand the operation." A low, howling autumn wind whipped through her as she glanced around the drive-in for any sign of Douglas or the girls returning. Nina pulled her knees to her chest for warmth. "It's tough to describe exactly, but the place is magical. It's also incredibly efficient. They've done an excellent job blending the vacation aspect with down-to-earth activities that forge connections."

"And has it rekindled your connection with Douglas?"

Lost in thought, she dimly registered a chorus of awws from the family closest to her as the dog on screen barreled toward her family. Nina toyed with the laces on her boots, wishing for her own version of the movie scene. Where all it took was love, will and movement to restore things between her and Douglas.

"Honestly, Ashlynn, it's difficult to tell. We're closer than we've been in a long while." And their sexual chemistry was off the chain. "But our core differences haven't changed."

A lump welled in her throat at the memory of her husband's refusal to be with her if there could be any possibility of a pregnancy. She understood his point since she'd argued for a divorce, of course. But the incident had been a painful reminder of that final argument that let her know there was no healing their marriage.

And speaking her doubts to Ashlynn made things more real. Tongue pressed to the inside of her front teeth, she inhaled deep, swallowing hard to push past the emotion threatening to swamp her.

Ashlynn said, "How are the girls doing?"

"They already suspect we've talked about getting divorced, which breaks my heart all over again—" Her voice cracked at their pain. If only she could shield them from the painful shards of a fracturing family.

"I'm so sorry they're hurting—and you as well," Ashlynn said softly, her voice full of compassion. "I wish there was something I could do."

She shifted on the blanket lining the truck bed, thinking how much warmer she'd been with Douglas beside her.

"Well, actually..." Now that the time had come to ask, she wondered if it was too much to expect from someone. She wasn't used to asking others for help. "I was wondering if your offer to watch the kids is still available?"

"Of course, it would be my joy." Her answer was immediate and full of authenticity. "I wouldn't have said it if I didn't mean it. I can come right away or this time next week and spend a couple of nights."

"Well, if you come now, you'll get to enjoy a vacation at the Top Dog Dude Ranch." Hopefully, that would make it less of an imposition.

"That would be amazing. I haven't had a vacation in over a year. So you would be doing me a favor, too."

How like Ashlynn to find a way to sound like Nina's request wasn't an imposition. "Well, there's certainly plenty to do here. I'll email you a list of what to pack."

"Perfect. Maybe I'll even meet the cowboy of my dreams while I'm there," she said with a grin in her voice. "Hey, my boss is waving for me, so I need to hang up. I'll look for your email and I'll message you with my ETA. Love ya."

"Love you, too. And thank you, so very much, for being there for me." She pushed aside a niggling voice in her head that questioned the wisdom of having sex with her husband after telling the twins they were splitting. She was in such uncharted territory here, it was tough to know what was best.

All she could do was follow her gut in the moment, and her gut was telling her that even if the marriage didn't work, they still related physically and what would it hurt to indulge that now that there wouldn't be any confusion about what it meant? It would be a welcome release, a chance to remember something good.

Scanning the crowd, she saw her husband and the twins approaching. Her eyes lingered on the hard lines of his face, his chiseled chest, soaking up the sight of him. She just hoped the time alone would give her the answers she needed. And if there weren't any answers? Then she would settle for closure, peace.

Douglas held the twins by the hands, moving at a breakneck speed. As she heard the movie ending, she realized how long they must have been gone. How odd that they weren't carrying any snacks.

And Douglas was clearly steaming mad.

Her stomach fell and her throat closed with anxiety. The ever-elusive peace she sought slipped even further away.

Douglas couldn't remember when he'd been so angry. He needed a dose of Nina's levelheaded parenting before he blew a gasket.

From twenty feet away, Douglas saw Nina pocket her phone into her tightly fitting jeans. Her face, even from this far away, was tense with confusion.

Boots stomping the dusty earth, Douglas held

on to his temper. Barely. He was still seeing red over finding his tomboy daughter batting her eyelashes at some scrawny boy who was looking at Kacie like… Douglas didn't want to follow that thought for one more second or his head would explode.

He charged past a family of four folding up their blankets from a place on the ground. The twins walked double-time beside him as he ate up the space on the way back to the truck with long strides. He prayed Nina would have the answers he needed for how to handle the girls.

When had Kacie become boy crazy? She was only ten years old.

He couldn't stomach the thought of his little girls growing up without him around. Boys coming to the house. It was all he could do not to scoop them up and keep them under lock and key until they were eighteen.

As Douglas closed the last few feet between him and his wife a round of applause sounded through the moviegoers as the last part of the credits blinked out. Car engines roared to life.

Nina hopped off the tailgate, her forehead creased with concern. "Douglas? Girls? What's going on?"

Kacie's jaw jutted with her signature stubborn nature.

Kelsey avoided their eyes and scrambled back up into the truck bed. She started folding the blanket with a level of concentration that far outstripped the task, clearly avoiding the conversation. He might as well let that slide, since she wasn't the offender.

This time.

"Kacie," he pressed, "do you want to tell your mother, or should I?"

Nina's eyes narrowed. "Tell me what?"

Kacie scuffed her toe in the dirt, a blush creeping up her face. "Feel free to tell her."

Kacie being shy? That was a new one. Douglas looked fast at Kelsey, wondering for a moment if somehow the girls had swapped places. It would make sense since he would have pegged Kelsey as the one to go boy crazy first. He checked for Kelsey's pierced ears and the tiny scar in Kacie's eyebrow. And there had been no swap. Kacie really was acting subdued.

"Kacie?" Nina asked. When their daughter still didn't answer, Nina turned to Douglas, voice level. "What happened?"

Douglas stared pointedly at Kacie, who still stayed silent.

Finally, Kelsey scooched closer. "She was flirting with a boy and Dad lost his cool."

Nina burst out laughing, looking so relieved

Douglas felt the anger rising all over again. How could she be so unconcerned?

"It's not funny," he insisted. "She's too young to be hanging out with boys. And even if that wasn't the case, we don't know the kid she was talking to. What if he was dangerous?"

Kacie fiddled with the hood strings on her sweatshirt. "I doubt he's a serial killer."

"Kacie," Nina cautioned.

"There were people everywhere. I'm not a baby." Kacie stood her ground, her eyes narrowing. "But maybe you and Mom should go off alone to talk about my punishment. Come on, Kelsey, let's walk back to the cabin."

Anger rippled through him all over again. Was she looking for another opportunity to sneak off to talk to that boy? "Not a chance, young lady. You two aren't stepping out of my sight."

"Dad," Kacie growled in exasperation. "You are embarrassing me. I was only talking to my new friends."

"Your new boyfriend," Kelsey teased.

"Boyfriend?" Nina asked, gathered, cool. Coaxing the story out of the twins with a finesse that he couldn't muster.

There was so much he couldn't afford to lose if she left him. He had to salvage something from the wreckage of their lives.

"He's a friend," Kacie said with exaggerated patience. "And he's a boy. It's not the same."

"Tell that to Dad." Kelsey snorted on a laugh, giving up the pretense of folding blankets now that the initial tension had diffused. She was all ears now.

Nina glanced at Douglas, then back at the girls. "What did he do?"

"He called me Doodle Bug. He hasn't called me that since I was four years old," she wailed, pressing her palms to her cheeks.

Kelsey bit her lip, a sad attempt at stifling a laugh as she clutched the forgotten quilt to her chest.

"It's not funny." Kacie stuffed her hands into the front pocket of her sweatshirt.

"Sure, whatever," Kelsey said, giggling.

Sighing, Kacie waved. "Come on, let's head back to the cabin." She glanced over her shoulder at her parents. "And yes, we'll stay within eyesight and we won't talk to anyone, especially boys. You and Dad can follow in the truck and discuss my punishment."

After wishing for time alone with his wife, he finally got it when he was in no shape to have a productive conversation. Right now, he was spoiling for a fight, a way to vent the frustration boiling inside him. Which would only hurt his case in winning his wife back.

"Girls," he barked. "Get in the truck. It's past my bedtime."

Sitting in the middle of the bed, Nina hugged her knees to her chest, watching Douglas move around their bedroom in the firelight. His low-slung sweatpants hugged his lean hips, his well-worn T-shirt stretching across broad shoulders and a muscular chest honed from a lifetime of farm work.

He looked delicious.

And she was starving.

He was also brooding and unapproachable as he stabbed at the logs in the grate.

The whole ride back from the drive-in movie, he'd been silent, radiating a "stand back" vibe. She would have been amused at his overprotective father act, except she needed to talk to him about her plan for Ashlynn to visit.

She thumbed a fraying seam on the quilt, looking for the words to put him in a more nostalgic frame of mind. "Remember when we both walked the floor all night long, each carrying a baby?"

"Which time?" He glanced back at her. "Because as I recall, we did that at least four times a week for at least six months."

At least he was talking.

"Any of the nights. Or all of them. You sang the rock tunes from your high school years, but in such a sweet voice the lyrics sounded like nursery rhymes."

Standing, he put the poker back in the metal bucket of fireplace tools. Flames crackled, brought to life by his careful attention. "I would have sung opera if it would have gotten them to sleep through the night."

Whimsy lit her insides at the notion. "Now that would have been entertaining."

He walked the room in his regular nighttime routine of checking the windows, making sure they were locked. "Remember the time we both woke up the next morning in a panic thinking something must be wrong with the girls since we slept so late?"

Memories of that long-ago spring morning swelled in her mind, of waking in bed with her husband feeling rested for the first time in... forever, it seemed. Warm sunlight had pierced the chiffon drapes, bathing her handsome husband in an amber glow. He'd rolled to kiss her, one of those unhurried early-morning embraces, only to stop short as they realized it was morning. And the baby monitor was quiet.

Calm had shifted to panic in a flash as they

scrambled to the twins' nursery, fearing the worst and finding…

"Tyler had them both, holding one cradled in each arm, watching the sports channel." The memory was so sweet, which made it all the more heartbreaking to remember. "He was good with them. He would have made a great father."

"He was a good father to me. A much better dad to me than I've been to the girls." Grief rolled off him in waves, his broad shoulders hunched as he stood at the window.

She shoved the quilt aside and swung her legs off the bed. Crossing to him, the wooden floorboards cold against her bare feet, she rested a hand on his back. "You're an amazing father. Why do you think I was open to having more?"

She'd had more time to think about that argument since they'd been at the ranch. More opportunity to consider why it had hurt so badly.

He looked over his shoulder at her, his jaw tight. "This isn't a subject—"

"Douglas, I hear you," she interrupted. "It's a loaded topic, and we both have strong feelings about it. Even if I don't agree, I respect your feelings on the subject."

"Since when?" he teased wryly, his mouth tipping into a half smile.

She eased to sit on the edge of his futon. "I've

been doing a lot of thinking lately. I don't mean to give you the impression I don't respect your opinions. That's just one of the reasons we have to figure out a way to deal with each other without all the tension in the air."

"Isn't that what we've been doing here at Top Dog?" He dropped to sit beside her, his thigh warm against hers.

She craved more of his touch. More of his heat. But she had to stay focused on the crisis at hand. For the sake of the girls. She took a breath, letting the air warmed by the fire fill her lungs.

"Not at all." She cast a sideways look at him, his face in the shadows of the flickering firelight. "We've been doing everything we can to avoid conflict, which just makes us explode and solves nothing."

"Well, then, what did you have in mind?" There was no missing the invitation in his voice or the blue-flame heat in his eyes.

The air thickened between them, the temperature in the room rising. It would be easy to lean in. Brush her lips to his. Let him run his hands all over her.

She swallowed hard against temptation, needing to keep the conversation on track. "A couple of things. First off, we need to stop delaying talking to the girls. It's no wonder they're on edge since we keep sending mixed signals."

"All right, that's fair." He crossed his arms over his chest. "When do you think is the right time?"

Never? Now? When would be a good time to tell children their parents were splitting? "Perhaps after the art therapy in the cave tomorrow? Kelsey's been looking forward to it and I'm worried if we chat beforehand, she might be too emotional. I would wait until we get home, but I'm afraid to put it off much longer for fear they'll figure out on their own. We need to be the ones to tell them."

His throat moved in a long swallow and Douglas stayed silent for so long she thought he might tell her no. Then a log dropped in the grate, shooting sparks, ending his stare.

He gave her a tight nod. "Sounds like a decent plan. I understand why we need to talk to them sooner rather than later. What's your second point?"

She hadn't expected this next part to be tougher. Scarier. Not because he frightened her, but because her mishmash of feelings for this man scared her. After her parents' deaths, uncertainty, change, turned out poorly more often than not.

But she knew this was too important to let fear rule her. "I think we need to spend time alone together, just the two of us, and deal with all of these feelings so we can co-parent peacefully. Which is also why I think we should talk to them tomorrow, so they don't misunderstand why we need time away."

His dark brows shot upward. "As much as I would love to take you up on that offer, how's it possible for us to be alone? We have the girls to consider."

"I called Ashlynn and asked if she can come to the ranch for the weekend. She can have the sofa bed in the great room."

His mouth tightened again, storm clouds gathering in his eyes. "You do realize that means we'll have even less time alone, right?"

Her heartbeat sped at just the thought of what she had planned. The alone time she craved. She hoped she was doing the right thing, for the right reasons. But whatever her reasoning, she knew that she and Douglas needed to spend more time talking through what was happening.

"Ashlynn would stay with the kids so we could take advantage of some couples-only options." She drew in a bracing breath and took the plunge. "We could even spend a night away, just the two of us, away from all the distractions."

If the temperature had spiked before, now the air turned charged between them, full of innuendo and need too long denied. She met his gaze fully, no hiding, no dodging, letting him see the hodgepodge of conflicted feelings inside her, including desire.

A desire she intended to act upon tomorrow, when she had him all to herself. All evening long until sunrise.

Standing, she backed to her cold, waiting bed. "Good night, Douglas."

Chapter Ten

Douglas hadn't expected to get such a fortunate break with Nina, especially not at her instigation. His luck had drained dry long ago. Or so he'd thought.

His wife had actually arranged for them to go away for a night alone together. He wasn't going to dwell overlong on the fact that they had to talk to the girls first. That was only wise in case things didn't turn out the way he wanted. Besides, they already suspected the marriage had been in trouble.

But things were looking up.

Whistling, he stood in the cabin's small kitchenette, equipped with basic food staples, and flipped a pancake. Since they weren't going to talk to the girls until after the cave painting class this afternoon, he figured he could make the most of their morning by reminding Nina of their old routine where he made breakfast on the weekends.

Inhaling scents of vanilla as he watched the pancake cook, some of the tension that had been mounting in his chest fell away from him. For the first time, he felt truly hopeful. Pancake sizzling in the cast-iron frying pan, his thoughts wandered. Imagining being tangled with Nina.

The sound of Nina in the shower set his mind on fire with images of her pale body lathered up with that lavender soap they'd made. Especially when he had the promise of a night alone with her, a possibility he'd hoped for, but never imagined she would be the one to instigate.

The chattering voices of his daughters broke his thoughts. Glancing over his shoulder toward the loft, he saw Kelsey's well-worn jeans first. She carefully climbed down the ladder singing in tune with Kacie. An old smartphone the girls used only for streaming music played a pop-country tune.

Kacie belted out lyrics about loving her horse and her dog, boots smacking into the ground. Kelsey held a hairbrush as a microphone as the twins made their way toward him.

The song ended and they both stuffed their hands into their respective front pockets of their hoodies. Both girls' clothes were old since they'd been instructed to pack items that could be thrown away if they got covered in clay and paint during the day's art activities. Kelsey's stained pale pink hooded sweatshirt boasted a unicorn with a flowing mane above the pocket. Kacie's dark green hoodie with a rip along the hem sported a herd of running horses on her back.

He appreciated the normalcy of the morning after the hard night with Kacie. He was grateful to see her behaving like a kid and—even better—getting along with her sister. They looked happy, a situation that lifted his spirits even more.

"Do you want your pancakes shaped like teddy bears or bunny rabbits?"

"Dad," Kelsey said primly, "I'm not a kid anymore."

Kacie raced to the stove, stretching up on her toes to look into the frying pan. "Well, I'm officially a kid for today so I'll take both Kelsey's rabbit and my bear."

"Coming right up." He poured circles of different sizes into the pan, the batter sizzling in the melted butter.

Kacie smiled up at him, her blue eyes twinkling. “Does this mean I’m forgiven for talking to that boy?”

He knew he should probably stand his ground, but his heart had been wrapped around their little fingers from the moment his daughters had been born.

Casting a sidelong look her way, he nodded reassurance. “You’re always forgiven. Just promise me you’ll be very careful. I need to be able to trust you.”

“Yes, sir.” She hugged him hard before skipping off to search the cabinets for syrup.

Thank goodness he could trust Ashlynn to watch over the kids like they were her own. The time she’d lived in the barn apartment, she’d been an invaluable help, a hard worker. He wished he could have found a way to afford to keep her on the payroll long term. Not just for the girls, but for Nina, too.

Had he tried hard enough, though?

Now wasn’t the time for second-guessing. He needed to focus on this window of opportunity with Nina. He didn’t have a boatload of money or fancy gifts to romance her.

But he was counting on the Top Dog magic to come through with inspiration before their date night began.

* * *

Nina was counting down the minutes until Ashlynn arrived to take the girls. Chewing the inside of her lip, she focused on calming her nerves with art therapy as they painted cave walls near the hot springs. Not much longer and she would be alone with her husband. Her foster sister had offered to take the girls in the past, and right now, Nina couldn't think of a reason why she hadn't accepted the offer sooner.

Camera in her leather bag at her feet, today she focused her artistic eye not on snapping pictures, but on adding stars to the painting on the sleek cave walls. The unique and broad canvas tapped into a whole new side to her creative spirit. Metallic silver flecks transformed the twilight-pink-and-periwinkle sky.

This time this art therapy was in its own sort of twilight. An appropriate ending for a day filled with creation. It almost calmed her taut nerves over talking to the girls.

Paintbrush grasped loosely between her fingertips, she cast a glance over her right shoulder to look for her daughters. The space echoed with the voices of other guests. Pottery from previous classes was scattered throughout, creating an eclectic space. Earlier today, Hollie had made a stunning vase in her tutorial. She made it look easy to form a balanced, sweeping vase.

From this angle and lighting, some of the pottery looked like stalagmites. Kacie's and Kelsey's mugs caught the midafternoon rays at the cave's mouth.

Turning her attention back to the cave wall, she felt a smile pull the corners of her lips skyward. She glanced at her family and at the sprawling mural they'd created together of the sweeping hills of Archer land. Not surprisingly, Kacie painted a horse. Kelsey worked on what looked like a young girl sitting beneath a tree reading. Douglas had surprised her with his attention to detail, from the barn to a bell around one of the cows' necks.

Nina had taken countless photos in her life, but there was something different, freeing about swiping paint along the cavern walls, images that might not be seen by anyone after today. This was for her. Just her. Moving down from the sky, she dipped her brush into the cobalt paint. She splashed paint across in a river of blue, like the waters that took her parents from her.

Her arm bumped against Douglas. His eyes locked with hers as he gathered the brushes right before he followed the girls deeper into the cave to the hot springs. A smile lit the space more effectively than the globes on the walls.

A snap of connection, like static, went all the way to her bones, filling her with wonder. Anticipation.

And a bucket of nerves.

Which seemed so silly after all this time. After everything. Still, she was ready to be alone with him, despite the fracture that was coming soon—too soon. He'd been so sweet about making pancakes this morning, serving up bears and rabbits like when the girls were little.

Small, fragile hope blossomed in her chest. She couldn't quite pin down the feeling.

Breathe in. Breathe out. She could do this.

Satisfied with their cave painting, she moved toward Douglas and the girls. They were cleaning the eco-friendly paint off in the hot springs, laughter resting easy in the air.

In no time at all, she closed the distance between them. Crouched next to Douglas. Let their legs touch. He didn't pull away. Instead, leaned into her with gentle pressure.

She tipped her head closer to his. "Need some help there?"

He shot a wry glance her way. "All my creativity got used up in pottery class." He pointed toward the cluster of pottery, gesturing to a lopsided vase painted purple. "Art never was my best subject. I meant for it to be blue, but the color mix was off. I added too much red apparently."

"I think it's precious."

"Good. Because it's for you." He chuckled, angling closer to her, his breath warm on her neck. "You don't have to look so horrified."

Nina's insides melted at the familiar heat of him, the steam from the springs giving life an ethereal haze.

"Not horrified. Just surprised." She could almost forget for a moment that they were going to talk to the girls soon about their plans to divorce.

She caught his eye again, his gaze direct, intense, no avoiding as he'd done too often in the past. A promise she wanted to cash as his mouth quirked. She felt her own lips part. Breath lodged in her throat.

"I made it thinking I would put wildflowers in it, for you. I haven't given you flowers near enough. I'm sorry for that. You deserve romance."

The world quieted around her, the silence cut only by the sounds of the bubbling water as she focused on him. Waiting for him to make a move, her heart pounded in her throat.

Douglas broke his eye contact, turning to look at Kacie, who tugged on his hand. She made a silly, scrunched face before bursting out with giggles.

Not surprising.

These moments between Douglas and her always seemed to be interrupted. There was no regret or surprise. But a mounting desire. Especially as their opportunities to be alone together would soon dwindle away completely. The urge to enjoy this time was almost overwhelming.

Kelsey flipped her hair over her shoulder. Seeming so grown already as she scooped up her backpack. "Did you have fun today, Dad? This was neat, wasn't it?"

"I guess your mom isn't the only artist in the family." Winking, Douglas held out the girls' jackets, then steered them toward the mouth of the cave.

Leaving behind the cave, the four of them set off on a nature hike down the mountain. Other art therapy participants milled around them, dispersing in the direction of their own cabins.

The woods were preternaturally still. As if the whole forest soaked in bronze afternoon light held its breath. Knowing that a shift in the fabric of everything was about to take place.

Steeling her nerve, Nina moved beside Douglas, her lips tight. He cocked his head to the side as she fixed him with a pointed look. She shoved her hands into her pockets. "I think our walk back would be a good time to have a family talk."

His smile faded and already she missed the ease of their day more than she could have imagined.

Douglas cleared his throat. "Girls, we need to talk to you."

Kacie gave them both a wary look. "About what?"

Kelsey stayed quiet, wrapping her arms around her stomach with a wince.

Nina swallowed, forcing air and light into her voice. She tried to stay calm, but the world seemed to spin. "You know your dad and I have been having trouble for a while."

The color drained from Kelsey's face.

A light breeze stirred the fallen leaves, sending squirrels skittering, their scampering the only sound in the forest aside from the crunching of twigs and pine straw beneath her family's feet.

Kacie's brow furrowed. "But things are better since we got here. This place is great."

Douglas put a hand on each girl's back. "It's been good to have a vacation as a family. We hope this trip has shown you that we will always be a family, even if we're having struggles in our relationship."

Kelsey wrapped her arms tighter around her stomach. "Please stop."

Nina stopped, cradling Kelsey's chin in her

hand. "Sweetie, this has nothing to do with how much we love you."

Kacie picked up a stick and chucked it into the tangle of branches ahead. "I knew it. I knew it! You two are getting divorced. Why did you even bother coming here if you'd already made up your minds?"

Nina's heart broke with every step she took. The world felt too big, too vast and open, reminding her too much of the day she'd realized she'd become an orphan. That her family could never be the same. Never be whole.

And if her girls were feeling even a fraction of that? Nina's stomach took a cliff dive.

Douglas jammed his hands into his jacket pockets. "We want you to see how we can all work together. We care about each other."

Kelsey's bottom lip trembled. "Why are you telling us this right now, Mom?"

"Sweetie, we need to spend some time alone planning for the future and we didn't want you two to get the wrong idea."

"Alone?" Kacie asked. "Where are we going?"

Nina knew she had to stay calm, stay in the moment. Even though her insides were a mess. "You girls are going to stay here in our cabin with Aunt Ashlynn for a while. She's joining us today."

Urgent and frantic birdsong added to the cacophony of sounds as they kept walking down the path.

Rubbing a hand along her forehead, Kelsey frowned, tears gathering in the corners of her eyes. "On our family vacation?"

"She's family, too," Nina reminded her gently. "My only family other than the three of you."

Douglas wrapped an arm around Kelsey, walking in step with her. Nina watched her daughter's shoulders sag just as their cabin crested into view. Though it looked decidedly less cozy when coupled with the wobbly tears falling down Kelsey's face, which Douglas stopped to wipe away.

He was such a good father. She would miss having him by her side to parent. For a moment, the promise of future pain from this split threatened to take her out at the knees. If only he could have been there for *her*, and not just for his daughters. She understood marriage changed a relationship, and she recognized that the twins had to come first for both of them. But she missed the tender affection she used to know at Douglas's hands. The care and concern when he looked into her eyes.

Lagging behind, Kacie snapped a twig off a nearby tree branch, the sound pulling Nina's thoughts back where it belonged. To her daughters and the hurt they had to bear that wasn't of their own making.

Kacie tugged another skinny branch. The bough bowed, sending leaves sailing to the ground. "You need to tell Aunt Ashlynn never mind. Things got out of hand yesterday. We were just trying to get you and Dad to work together. I thought Dad would get mad if I was talking to a boy and race straight to you—and I was right."

Was everything the girls had done part of an elaborate subterfuge? She'd guessed goat yoga had been selected to keep them close. But flirting with a boy to force them to talk seemed like a whole new grand-master level.

Nina's eyes sought her husband's, their gazes meeting. Holding. And wasn't this a kind of communication, too? She hated that Douglas didn't talk to her more. But she couldn't deny they shared another language. One, perhaps, that she didn't give enough credit for connecting them.

She cleared her throat, attention shifting back to Kacie. "If you got what you wanted, then why are you so upset now?"

"Because everything's messed up. You two are quitting." Her daughter looked at the ground, scuffing a worn tennis shoe through the leaves. "And I miss my sister. She asked me why I hate her, and I don't. I know I pick on her, but I can't seem to stop myself. I'm just so mad all the time. You wouldn't understand."

Nina's heart plummeted to think her rocky marriage had done that to her daughter—giving her cause to feel angry that way. She understood better than her daughter could imagine. She hooked an arm around Kacie's shoulders and hugged her against her side. "A sister is a very special friend. I miss mine, too."

And as if Ashlynn had somehow heard the plea to be there right that minute, her squeal carried on the breeze along with Kelsey's and Douglas's greetings. Ashlynn waved, a broad sweeping gesture that held so much casual grace and elegance. The sight of her sister dressed in a plaid shirt and skinny jeans picking her way toward them threatened Nina's tenuous grip on keeping it together.

Her sister's long, loose curls cascaded down her back, her smile every bit as familiar and welcoming as it had been that first day Nina pulled up to her latest foster home. Nina sprinted, boots hitting the ground as she wrapped Ashlynn in a deep hug.

Needing her support now more than ever.

Watching Ashlynn wrap Nina in a tight hug, the two women rocking back and forth, Douglas saw firsthand how disconnected and alone Nina had been in these past few years. True, he'd known the bond between Nina and Ashlynn ran deep and true, but Nina's body language now spoke other stories. Told of wounds of isolation.

And that socked him in the gut when he was already reeling from the hurts he'd doled out to the twins just now. He squeezed Kelsey's shoulder once more, remembering her tears and hating that he'd put them there. Bad enough that the girls were upset. Now he was witnessing for himself how badly he'd failed with Nina that she needed her sister so much it was evident to anyone looking at them.

Finally, Nina loosened her grip on her sister and let out a pained, almost manic bark of laughter. Nina placed a hand to her temple and shook her head in what seemed to be a combination of disbelief, shock and relief.

How had she become so isolated? How had this happened beneath the roof of their home?

If he could win her back…

No.

That wasn't right. *When* he won her back, he'd never let her feel so alone again. Never let Nina revisit this place of loneliness.

Stepping forward to carry Ashlynn's overnight bag, Douglas opened the cabin door. With a resounding creak, the door swung inward. He nodded, a motion for everyone to step through the threshold, watching as his family plastered on welcoming smiles. "Thank you for coming so quickly, Ashlynn."

"I can't wait to spoil them rotten." She pulled two bags of sour gummies from her purse and passed them to the girls trailing her into the main living area. "I've been trying to visit for the longest time. It was serendipity that things worked out."

Kacie shook her head, hands working to open the sour gummy pack. "It's Top Dog magic."

Ashlynn looked from Douglas to Nina before returning her attention to the twins. "What do you mean?"

Kelsey gave a soft smile. "Oh, you'll see."

Douglas wasn't content to leave this evening up to chance—or magic. He intended to stack the deck in his favor in every way possible. "If you ladies are okay to hang out alone for a while, I have some errands to run."

Nerves tapping overtime in her stomach, Nina pulled out the smaller of their suitcases, finally alone with Ashlynn to have a talk without worries anyone would overhear.

The twins were in the loft. Kacie had been polishing her boots, wanting them to look just perfect for their next horse-based activity while Kelsey continued reading her chapter book. At least she'd been afforded this small luxury. One-on-one time with her sister as she packed for the mystery outing Douglas was planning.

Every moment she spent with Ashlynn made it hard to remember they hadn't always been sisters. The space between them had always been comfortable, knowing.

Dropping onto the futon, Nina slumped next to her sister, breathing in her jasmine-scented perfume. The same perfume she'd been wearing since they were teens. "I can't believe you got here so fast. You must have left right after we hung up."

She shrugged, holding up one of Nina's shirt options. She shook her head, curls shaking in slight dismissal of the potential outfit. "Not too long thereafter. I didn't need to pack very much, and my neighbor is taking care of the cat."

"How's Miss Kitty doing?" Nina held up another shirt, a silent question for approval.

Ashlynn nodded and the shirt went into another pile of maybes.

"Fat as ever." Ashlynn leaned forward, elbows on her knees. "But I'm more interested in hearing how you're doing."

Standing, Nina tugged open one of the drawers on the antique dresser, wishing she had brought prettier underwear. She dug around, pulling out a matching bra and panties set, white with a hint of lace. Passable, but not ideal. When leaving the farm, she hadn't expected sex to be on the agenda. "When we decided to come here, I was certain Douglas and I were over. We even told the girls as much today."

A conversation that had pierced her heart, an ache that lingered still.

"But you're not certain?"

Wasn't she? This time here at the Top Dog Dude Ranch had been every bit as magical as advertised. It had made her see what her family could be—how her husband could be—and that made her wonder. Was there a possibility he could change? And yes, that she could, too? She only knew one thing for certain.

"I know we can't continue on as we have been. Except..." Nina's voice trailed off. She let her mind wander, recalling the heat in Douglas's eyes.

Ashlynn tipped her head into Nina's line of sight. "Except what?"

She sagged against the dresser. "Except I can't help but wish we could go back to the way things were."

"You're smarter now. Maybe it can be better this time," Ashlynn said, ever the optimist no matter what life threw at her.

Nina winced. "I told myself that more than once."

She picked at one of her cuticles on her manicured hand. “Sounds to me like you’re still hoping or you wouldn’t be going off with him.”

Did Ashlynn always have to be right? Of course Nina was hoping. But she also had to be a realist, for her daughters’ sake. “We have to find a way to hold on to the peace we’ve found here even after we leave, for the girls.”

“And if you can’t?”

Even if she didn’t have the prettiest, laciest underwear packed, she was going to take what she could from this night with Douglas. “Then I hope I get one last chance to make love with my husband before we walk away.”

Chapter Eleven

Anticipation coursing through his veins, Douglas draped his wrist over the steering wheel, pressing the accelerator as they sped along the weaving mountain road. The sun setting into the valley cast a warm haze over trees already ablaze with autumn colors. He'd been driving in convoluted circles for a while, hoping she wouldn't guess where they were headed.

He'd made the most of the afternoon planning the perfect evening getaway, with more than a little help from Jacob O'Brien. Initially, he'd thought about a night in downtown Gatlinburg, but that felt too much like a date and he was afraid she would bolt. So he opted for a dinner in what he hoped was a romantic place, but if she wasn't in that frame of mind, she would just see it as a secluded location to talk.

Toying with one silver hoop earring, she stretched long legs encased in black jeans until her feet were under the heater. "I'm eaten up with curiosity over where we're going."

Glancing in the rearview, he guided the vehicle carefully around a hairpin turn. "You've always said you like surprises and I'm finally stepping up."

"Fair enough. Thank you for taking the reins to plan this so I could spend more time with Ashlynn and packing. I can't think when's the last time you and I have had a night away from the girls. It will be good for us to have a chance to, uhm, talk."

Her voice flared with a husky heat he really hoped he wasn't misreading.

"Have you heard anything from Ashlynn about how the girls are doing?" With another fluid turn, Douglas led them toward their final destination and his big move.

"They've already packed the schedule full and texted me the details." She pulled her phone out of her large leather bag. "Tonight, they're taking a wagon ride through the ranch with stargazing. And tomorrow morning they're going zip-lining."

"Kelsey's going zip-lining?" He chuckled. "I can't imagine that making her top ten list of things to do."

She leaned her head against the glass, her hand gravitating to the camera in her large leather purse, as he knew she did when nervous.

"Probably not even her top hundred. Kacie insisted the debt still hasn't been repaid for going to goat yoga."

"I'm glad Ashlynn was able to help on such short notice." And the fact that Nina had asked her? Hope grew. "Will she be able to stay after we get back tomorrow so you two can visit? I know you miss her."

"I do, so much." She drew an absent circle with her finger on the passenger window.

The town glittered in a valley below, the mountainside speckled with stray lights. Beautiful. But not even close to being as lovely as his wife in profile.

Douglas tapped a finger on the steering wheel in time with the song whispering through the radio. "I'm sorry I didn't make a point to include Ashlynn in our lives more often."

Nina turned back to him. "She lived with us for six months."

"And that time was the happiest I've ever seen you." As he said the words, he realized he hadn't really registered that fact before. What else had he missed, too preoccupied with keeping the farm together during his brother's illness? "I'm sorry to have isolated you so much."

Her face softened and she squeezed his arm, lingering. "We've both had such full plates there hasn't been much time to think or analyze. For what it's worth, I don't blame you for our problems. Life just dealt us both an unrelenting hard hand."

"We aren't the only ones." Their girls were affected by this.

Nodding knowingly, she absently skimmed her fingers along his wrist. "So, we haven't had time to talk about Kacie and her boy crush. Do you really believe she was only talking to him to make you angry?"

"I don't know. God help me, I'm not ready for this. Shouldn't they still be debating what Halloween costume they're going to wear this year?" Kacie's sudden interest in boys reminded him time moved forward and would continue to move forward without him if he and Nina split.

"I would guess Kacie doesn't think it has to be a choice between boys and a Halloween costume."

Tension knotted in his gut. "What did she tell you?"

"Initially she may have talked to the boy to

get your attention so we would have to talk, but then… I get the impression she started enjoying the conversation." Her grip tightened on his hand, comforting.

"Great," he said with a growl, already tired of this topic. Thank goodness they were approaching the location for his date night to woo his wife. "I thought we had a while longer before this stage hit."

"I'm sure she was just testing the waters. We'll keep an eye on her, but we can't prevent her from growing up."

"Okay, I hear you," he agreed. He put the car in Park in front and turned to his wife.

Her eyes went wide, and she opened her mouth for what he was certain would be an argument. He leaned over and pressed a quieting kiss to her lips, his hands clasping her arms gently, savoring the soft give of her under his touch.

"Nina, tonight is for you, about you. You call the shots. Do you understand what I mean?" He would never push her. He simply wanted tonight to be whatever she chose. Whatever she needed. He wasn't much of a communicator, but he would make sure she understood that.

Her eyes flared with warmth. She cradled his face in her hands. "Completely. Attraction has never been our issue. We just have to figure out how we are going to deal with it going forward," she said, always so good at cutting straight through to what mattered. "Even if—when—we have sex tonight, that doesn't change anything between us."

He chose to ignore the part about nothing changing and focus on the fact she was open to having sex. He knew what tonight was about and he'd put his best foot forward in planning. "Do you trust me?"

She studied him with a gaze that pierced to his core. To his soul.

"Actually, Douglas, yes, I do."

Relief flooded him and he realized her answer, her trust, mattered so much more than he'd realized. He needed to know he hadn't failed her, that she believed he could come through for her and the girls. Even if he couldn't deliver the dream they'd once shared, at least he could build a new one.

Starting tonight. Stakes were high, and as his brother would have said, he was swinging for the fences.

Nina held her hands out in front of her, the blindfold covering her eyes, Douglas's strong hands on her shoulders, guiding her along some kind of dirt path.

"Careful," he said. "There's a big root. Go right. Now step up onto the sidewalk."

She inched her foot forward until she found the end of the concrete. "Oh my goodness," she said, grimacing, "please say there aren't people watching me stumble around."

"I wouldn't do that to you. I promise that your dignity is intact. We are completely alone."

A shiver of anticipation tingled up her spine. She breathed in deeply to steady her racing pulse… and smelled sulfur? "Are we near the cave?"

"Actually," he said, swiping off the face mask, "we are inside the cave."

The space sprawled before her lit by dim lights recessed in stone, showcasing their artwork from earlier with the springs bubbling in the distance. A pile of pillows was stacked Bohemian-style beside the steaming waters. A round table with two chairs had been set up as well. Covered in a white tablecloth, it had been set with china and candles. A cart was parked beside it, laden with covered dishes.

She barely knew what to say. It was such a sweet and romantic gesture. "You did this? For me?"

"For both of us." He held out his hands. "May I take your coat, madam?"

"Yes, sir, you may."

As he pulled her jean jacket off, his hands slid down her arms in a slow glide that brought goose bumps under her silky sweater. Her toes curled in her leather boots.

Dinner could wait. “Do you think our food would keep while we go back to the truck to, uhm, make out?”

A slow smile spread over his face and he stepped closer, his hips so very close. “Why go to the truck? We have our own sauna right here.”

Surprise sizzled through her, along with a hefty dose of desire. Her husband wasn’t impulsive, or rather, she hadn’t thought so. She’d been wrong. Tonight was all about following impulse to see what feelings still lived within them, and how to find balance for that before the real world full of responsibilities intruded again.

He’d understood better than she gave him credit for. Tenderness stirred, an affection threaded through the desire. Whereas once she would have embraced that half of the equation—the roots of their old love—now she needed to lean in to the physical. To savor the part of their relationship that wouldn’t break her heart again.

“Are you sure no one will walk in on us?” She slid her arms around his neck, toying with his hair.

“Absolutely certain.” He nodded without hesitation. “There’s no way I would leave you vulnerable that way. I planned out this evening with Jacob’s help—including reserving the springs. We have the place to ourselves until midnight."

"And afterward?" Her hands glided to his shoulders, digging into the muscles rippling under her fingertips.

His eyes lit with a mesmerizing blue flame. "We have the use of an empty cabin and just need to vacate by noon."

"That's a lot of time for…talking," she teased with a smile. "Do you think you're up to the task?"

A husky laugh rumbled from him as he skimmed his mouth over her lips, along her jaw, down to the pulse in her neck. "I do like it when you talk to me."

"Oh, really?" she moaned, tipping her head, giving him better access. "Well, for when we get to the time where talking stops, I brought condoms."

He angled away, lifting an eyebrow. "I did as well."

She gave herself two heartbeats to digest his words on what had been such a flash point for them in the past, then she decided to let it go for now. "Then we'll be well set for the night."

Done with talking, she cupped the back of his head and urged him in for another kiss, a full kiss, open mouths and sweeping tongues. As much as she'd tried to tell herself she was looking for level ground for the sake of their children, she couldn't deny this night was for her. She'd lost so much, she needed—deserved—to capture this memory with Douglas, regardless of where it led afterward.

Walking her backward, he eased her into a chair at the table and knelt in front of her to unzip one of her boots, his fingers trailing along her leg as he tugged. Then the other boot and another delicious stroke that ramped anticipation higher. Hotter. Made all the more intense by the utter isolation of the cave, the rest of the world and worries so very far removed.

She looked down the length of her leg at him while peeling her sweater up and over her head. "One of us is still way overdressed."

She flung the pink angora aside, reveling in how his eyes took in her white lace bra. While she'd mourned not bringing racier lingerie, she still felt utterly delicious, completely desirable in his eyes. She swayed forward to pluck at the buttons on his chambray shirt.

He covered her hands with his and helped speed the process. "Someone's impatient."

"Someone's—I'm—also done with talking." She stood slowly, hooking her thumbs in her jeans and with deliberate precision sliding the front button free.

His gaze went molten hot and he stripped off the rest of his clothes without looking away from her for even an instant. Denim, cotton and lace landed in a haphazard array on the rocky slab until they stood in front of each other, bare. She soaked in the sight of him, bronzed muscle and man. Hers.

For the first time in months, they were going to have sex.

How could it have been that long since they'd been intimate? She'd never imagined they would be that couple who drifted apart…

She stopped that thought short before it stole this night from her.

Clasping hands with her, he stepped into the bubbling waters, leading her, the heat easing over her flesh like delicious silk until it lapped around her legs, her hips, her breasts. Douglas stood in front of her, arms sliding around her waist and cupping her bottom to pull her closer. So close the heat of his arousal pressed against her stomach as they sank deeper into the pool.

She needed this. Needed him.

Maybe he felt the same way about her, because their kisses took on a frenzied edge, hunger billowing as tangibly as the steam rising from the churning waters. This moment, this man, was the stuff of fantasies. Her fantasies. And she didn't linger overlong on the thought, losing herself in the now, in the timelessness of the cavern and the thoughtfulness of his choice to bring her here.

The waters felt healing, like they washed away the hurts of the past and bathed them in new opportunities to connect. Such a beautiful sensation.

As he walked backward, he drew her with him, each step teasing her senses as their bodies shifted together. His strong thighs grazing hers. The hard planes of his chest teasing her aching breasts. A needy whimper escaped her, and he answered her by drawing her deep into the water with him until he sat on a step, bringing her to rest in his lap.

Straddling him, she moved closer, as close as she could get while still not nearly enough. Her fingers glided over his glistening muscles, steam rising around his body, outlining his powerful frame in the mist. She wished they could just finish this right here, right now.

But they needed birth control. "Let's move this to shore."

His growl of agreement rumbled low in his throat and he hooked an arm around her waist. Standing, he lifted her with him, water beading down and off her body. He carried her with powerful ease, his strength made all the more thrilling for the way he tempered it with gentleness.

He stretched her out onto the pile of cushions, covering her with his heat. His roughened body was a gentle, tempting abrasion against her skin. His caress aroused her in the way of a lover who knew her body well, teasing along her breast, leaving a lingering kiss on the sensitive inside crook of her elbow. And more, so much more.

She'd missed him, missed being with him, and didn't intend to waste a moment together, reciprocating touch for touch, temptation for temptation. Skimming a foot along his calf, she arched up with impatience and stretched out a hand to search for her purse without breaking what had to be the best kiss of her life.

"Nina," he whispered against her lips. "I've got it."

His hand slid from her hip for an instant before coming back with a condom. She didn't even care where he'd stashed it; she was just relieved they didn't need to stop.

She plucked the packet from his palm and sheathed him, taking a moment to enjoy the heat and length of him. He eased into her with such beautiful familiarity it brought tears to her eyes.

And then he moved and rational thought scattered, replaced by passion, a driving desire for more of him, more of this, however long it lasted. She stored sensations and memories, steam floating over them, slicking between them as she sank further into the pillows and sensation.

The need gathered tighter and tighter inside her,

her heart pounding. Each breath heavier and faster than the last until…

She flew apart, unraveling in his arms, locking her heels around his waist to hold on to the pulsing sensations as long possible. His hoarse shout of completion echoed in the cave along with her own. She clutched him tighter, all the while knowing that no matter how hard she held on, he was already slipping away.

Dread had been skipping rocks across her stomach all morning since Kelsey woke up to Aunt Ashlynn's eggs-and-bacon breakfast. It wasn't that the food had been bad. In fact, she loved her aunt's cooking. It was that with each bite she kept thinking about what would happen after she finished.

Zip-lining.

Shivering in spite of her jacket over her sweatshirt, she trailed behind her aunt and fearless Kacie on the wooded path to the zip-line area. Kelsey toyed with the safety harness, playing with the slack in her right hand.

She'd barely slept after the wagon ride and stargazing. Her mind had been so full of worries about how things were going for her parents, it was all she could do not to throw up. She didn't know how much longer she could hide her symptoms from her parents. Why couldn't they just figure out their problems and love each other again?

Kelsey tried to steady her breathing, drawing in deep gulps of mountain air, and exhaling slowly the way her teacher had taught her to do when she got stressed before a test. Kacie never needed to breathe into a bag to calm down. Kacie was the bravest person she knew.

Kacie skipped ahead, waving to the boy from the night at the drive-in movie. Her twin fell into easy conversation with the skinny, brown-haired fellow. Dad would blow a gasket. Kelsey tugged her sleeves down over her hands.

Ashlynn placed a hand on Kelsey's back, cutting through her thoughts. She looked at her aunt, wondering if she'd guessed how upset Kelsey was, in spite of trying to hide her nerves. Aunt Ashlynn was like Kacie. Fearless and bold. Aunt Ashlynn adjusted her own harness, which somehow looked cute atop her deep white V-neck with billowy sleeves, black leggings and brown leather boots.

"Here, kiddo." Ashlynn offered her a pair of gloves. "It should warm up soon."

"Thanks." She took the black wool gloves and tugged them on.

Ashlynn kept pace alongside her. "Is something on your mind?"

She shook her head. "I'm just nervous about zip-lining. My stomach hurts."

"Are you sure that's all? There can be more than one worry on a person's mind at a time. Even little things can build up into a big something until you don't feel good at all."

Kelsey looked ahead at the activity station coming closer with each step. She gulped, looking at the first hurdle she would have to overcome. Zip-lining. Then her mom and dad's divorce.

Then all her symptoms and her illness.

"Or sometimes it can be a big thing and you're really sick."

Ashlynn paused for a step before walking again. "Would you like to talk about it? That can help."

Nothing was going to make the pain go away. She'd researched all of her symptoms on the internet. But she needed to tell Aunt Ashlynn something. "I'm worried about my mom and my dad. You probably know why since you and Mom tell each other everything."

"I'm here to see you girls and give your parents time alone to talk."

"Talk?" Kelsey snorted, so frustrated and angry and hurt she could scream or cry. Or both. "All they do is talk and fight. Or ignore each other, which is just as bad."

Her voice cracked, her chest going tight. But she took another breath and pressed on.

"When adults say 'we'll always be a family no matter what,' that's just code. I've heard enough of my friends at school share about their parents' breakups to know that really means they're splitting and the kids are going to be shuttled back and forth between houses."

Ashlynn swept back a strand of hair that had fallen loose from Kelsey's braid and tucked it behind her ear. "That must sound really scary."

Kelsey flinched away from her touch, angry at the world. "What would you know about that?"

Ashlynn looked at her in surprise. "Are you really asking me that question? I grew up in foster homes with strangers."

"Oh, uh, I'm sorry?" Her face went hot with humiliation. How could she have been so self-centered? Her head started hurting. She just wanted to run back to the cabin and crawl under the covers for the day and read a book.

"It's okay. I understand how when you're in the middle of something painful it's hard to see what others are feeling."

"Was foster care that bad?" She knew her mom had been in foster homes, but she never talked about it much. She said it was in the past.

"I wasn't abused, if that's what you're asking,"

she said gently. "But yeah, it was scary not knowing what might happen next and when I could be moving."

Kelsey kicked at a cluster of dried leaves, launching them into the brisk breeze. "Our mom lived that way as a teenager."

"I remember. It was a good day for me when she came into my life."

Kelsey nodded toward her sister skipping alongside the boy. "She loves the farm. She kept telling Dad they could save it if he just wouldn't give up. He said she wasn't being realistic."

"I didn't realize it was your mom who wanted to hang on to the farm." Ashlynn swept aside a low-hanging branch, then stepped to the end of the line of people. "I always assumed it was your dad."

"I thought you two told each other everything."

"Sometimes we hear what we assume and get all worked up only to find out we totally misunderstood."

"Well, that's not a problem for people like you and Kacie."

Pausing, Ashlynn stepped over a rotten log. "Well, that's where you would be wrong."

"Really?" Kelsey asked, arms wrapping around her chest in a self-hug.

"I was absolutely terrified when I got to my first foster home. I was eight. Not much younger than you, actually. All the sounds and smells were strange. I cried myself to sleep and woke up crying all over again. My stomach hurt so badly I couldn't eat for days."

"I bet you were worried you were sick, sometimes, or, uh, that maybe you were going to die." Kelsey looked at her aunt. "What did you do?"

"Well, my foster mom took me to the doctor only to be told there was nothing wrong with me. But my stomach was still so upset, night after night. Then one of the older foster kids handed me a stuffed animal and taught me how to calm down by using my five senses—think of five things you see, five things you hear, and so on. It helped me keep perspective and slow my brain down when I felt overwhelmed. It still does."

Kelsey filed away the idea, curious about it but unable to fully appreciate what Aunt Ashlynn said as they shuffled closer to the zip line. Whoops of terror and excitement carried on the breeze.

Her aunt continued speaking, her relaxed tone reminding Kelsey that she was the only frightened one in their group this morning. "When your mom arrived at our foster home, she was terrified, too. But I could tell we were destined to meet each other, to become sisters. As soon as we started talking, I felt like I had known her my whole life."

"Mom says that about you, too." Kelsey inched

forward in the line, glad to have something else to think about.

"So I knew I had to help her get settled. I showed her where all the good junk food was stashed. Gave her lots of hugs when things at school were going awful. I just…made sure I was there. And she did the same for me. It wasn't all sunshine, but having each other to lean on helped. Do you understand what I'm saying?"

"That family is important?"

"Yes, that's the first part. The second part is accepting their help and comfort."

Kelsey churned the words over in her brain. She prided herself on logic and facts and being in control. But this? What Aunt Ashlynn had told her? It was about letting other people have control, which was scary, too.

Locked in thought, Kelsey moved toward the zip line waiting line. Nerves cranking again, she figured she had nothing to lose by trying something different. By taking Aunt Ashlynn's advice and letting someone else guide her through something frightening.

So she counted five things she saw…a brown bird in the tree, the instructor's bright orange vest, a pile of gray rocks stacked in the stream—

Suddenly, Ashlynn's arm shot out and brought her up short.

"Kelsey, stop," she cautioned softly but with undeniable intensity.

A big, skinny mongrel stood in front of a bush, teeth bared. Growling. Hackles raised. Not at all one of the friendly Top Dog canines. This was an animal in full defensive mode.

Then she heard it, the other, softer noises. Tiny little yips and squeaks coming from the underbrush nearby. She took a closer look back at the furry beast and realized all that hair almost covered milk-filled teats.

And then she realized, the dog wasn't mean and aggressive. The mama was protecting her litter of puppies.

Chapter Twelve

With the final minutes ticking away until they had to leave the little getaway cabin at noon, Douglas drew his wife to his side, both of them naked under the quilt. Her soft body pressed against him as she rested her head on his chest as they took a catnap after waking up to make love again. He breathed in the scent of her hair. He'd missed sharing a bed with her, the scent of their lovemaking around them.

No matter how much he had of Nina—whether it was sex or just holding her—he never could get enough. He skimmed a hand up and down her spine, sated for now, hoping their time away had been enough to earn him a second chance.

Or at the very least, a chance at a second chance.

After they'd made love in the cave, they'd packed up their meal. Dinner had been decadent. Rosemary and garlic-encrusted prime rib. Mashed potatoes with creamy gravy. Butter-soaked green beans. Red wine he tasted on Nina's tongue as they kissed before they'd driven to their getaway cabin. Dishes huddled together on the green painted dresser, messy stacks testifying to the aftermath of late-night snacking. He was especially pleased with the dessert choice, something called a mountain stack cake, steeped in an old tradition when guests would each bring a layer. She'd smiled so beautifully when he'd told her, he felt like he'd won the lottery.

Unlike the cabin he, Nina, and the girls had been sharing, this one-room space boasted intimacy, a sentiment reinforced by how the pale morning light bounced off the pine wood walls. Scents of apple and cinnamon permeated the air, coming from the wax burner shaped like a puppy. The quaint atmosphere reminded him of the bachelor pad over the barn where his brother had lived, the same space where Ashlynn had stayed for six months.

Thank goodness for Ashlynn watching the kids and making the date night possible. He wondered if he could persuade her to leave North Carolina and move back to the farm— He stopped that thought short. Was he honestly considering keeping the place after all?

Even the possibility stirred a wary hope in him he wasn't sure he was ready to consider. It felt too…perfect. It felt like a dream he'd already released once, and it nearly killed him. How could he manage a loss like that again if he couldn't figure out a way to keep the place for good?

Nina traced circles with her fingers along his chest. "Thank you for planning everything. It was good to get away."

"I wish I had done something like this sooner." He cupped her bottom and pulled her closer.

She slung a smooth leg over his, smiling with a hint of languid seduction in her amber-brown eyes. "We're not out of time yet."

Chuckling, he dropped a lingering kiss on her lips, indulging himself in a leisurely caress of her beautiful breasts. Even more than he wanted to keep the farm, he wanted more of these lazy mornings in bed with her. He should have recognized that earlier. Put her first sooner.

If he was going to make that happen, he would need to woo her with more than sex. He needed to dig deep, deeper than he'd ever imagined possible to give her what she wanted. Trying to be romantic, more open. Stepping out on a limb like this was scary, the stakes higher than ever if he failed.

Nina shifted under the covers. "I'm not sure when there would have been time back home."

Dig deep, he reminded himself. "I should have figured it out. I was just so worried—" *afraid* "—that something bad would happen if I was away."

"You aren't responsible for every bad thing that happens in the world." Natural light filtering in through the limbs of nearby trees cast her warm brown eyes in tender shadows.

"And to think we were sure everything would be perfect if the twins just survived." He scrubbed a hand along his chest, right over where his heart squeezed. "But I saw them and kept thinking how my parents died and here I was about to lose my children."

Sometimes, the bitterness of hope wrecked him. The idea that once this storm passed, everything would just work out. They'd suffered through enough.

"I didn't know you were feeling that then." She tipped her face up to look at him, stroking his cheek. "I'm sorry I couldn't step outside of my own fears enough to see yours so we could comfort each other."

Before he could stop himself, the words poured out. "Just when I felt like I was getting my feet under me again, losing Tyler brought back the full weight of those memories crashing down."

Her fingers stilled on his jaw. "Why didn't you tell me you were feeling this way when we were losing Tyler? Or afterward?"

Because sharing that piece of himself might have cracked him wide-open. It had been all he could do to get up every day to take care of the farm and his family.

"I'm telling you now," he said carefully instead. "Is it too late?"

Time paused. He could hear the steady tick-tick-tick of the wrought iron clock on the wall across from the bed.

"I don't know. I honestly don't." She looked away, as if meeting his eyes could offer an invitation she wasn't willing to extend. "I do know I can't even consider a future together if the next time we have a crisis in our lives you shut down altogether. Maybe we can get lifetime membership cards to the Top Dog Dude Ranch."

"That's not funny."

She shot a sidelong glance at him. "Sure it is, a little bit at least."

"Okay, maybe a little." Especially if that meant they would still be coming as a family. His heart knocked against his rib cage. Relief tangled up with all the other feelings roiling in his gut at dredging up old memories and yes, even the good stuff from being with Nina through the night.

God, he hoped this emotional purging paid off because he was gutted, depleted. He didn't have another word left to offer her. Usually when he felt twitchy like this, he found something to fix on the farm. If Nina had been right about what he needed to do to rekindle their relationship, could she also be on the mark that he may have overlooked a way to save their home and livelihood?

The chime of an incoming text pulled him back from his thoughts. He'd put his phone on Do Not Disturb, only allowing for three numbers to push through that setting.

Jacob O'Brien and Ashlynn, in case there was an emergency with the girls.

And the Jacksons, for if there was a problem at the farm.

Both scenarios made his stomach clench.

Dread dropped him back into the realities of his daily life and he angled away to grab his cell off the bedside table. "I should get that. It could be about the kids."

Nina placed a hand between his shoulder blades. "Is it the kids?"

Sitting up straighter, he pulled open the text... His stomach dropped. "No, it's the Jacksons back home. There's a problem at the farm."

* * *

Braiding her hair, Nina braced her boots against the truck's floorboards as they jostled over a pothole in the mountain road. Once that text came through, there hadn't been time to shower—or talk. They'd just thrown on their clothes and dashed out the door.

How different things had felt in the seat of their pickup fourteen hours ago. Memories of their time in the cabin stirred phantom sensations of longing. Her husband's roving hands across her thighs. Her need to touch him. Their closeness, a connection she hadn't felt in longer than she cared to admit.

And today?

A quick glance to the driver's seat gave Nina the sensation of free-falling, stomach dropping level after level with no parachute to deploy. Nina watched Douglas as he thumbed his phone, eyes half on the brightly lit screen as he turned into the driveway for the cabin. Worry knit his brows together, causing hard lines to surface in his forehead and around the edges of his eyes.

Douglas had become distant after the text, even more so after calling the Jacksons. She recognized his mood. He was more than withdrawn. He'd shut down altogether. Their fantasy evening was over and reality was back in full force.

One brief message about broken machinery was

all it had taken for Douglas to bolt out of bed and insist they head back to the Top Dog Dude Ranch. She had to confess, she was nervous, too.

His cell phone rang right as he pulled the truck alongside Ashlynn's compact car.

"It's the Jacksons again," he said brusquely before answering. "Yeah, hello?" Douglas's baritone voice filled the truck cab as he turned off the engine.

The girls waved from the cabin window, blissfully unaware of the latest struggle in their parents' rocky marriage. Kacie and Kelsey rushed out the cabin door, chattering excitedly. Douglas held a finger to his lips, waving them off toward Nina. Worry radiated from him in waves.

"So can you tell me more?" Douglas said, blue eyes widening as he made his way around the back of the cabin to continue his call.

Kelsey and Kacie tugged on Nina's red sweater, leading her inside. But her mind was half out of the cabin, panic and worry igniting her steps. She did her best to take a steadying breath before crossing the threshold.

Ashlynn sat at the small, squat table where she did an exaggerated point toward a plate piled high with what smelled like fresh-baked sugar and chocolate chip cookies. Through the window, she could see Douglas pacing around the yard on his cell phone. Thank goodness the kids didn't notice.

Kelsey waved a sugar cookie in the air excitedly. "Did you two have fun? We had a blast last night on the wagon ride and stargazing."

Kacie trailed her sister. "Kelsey was really good at naming the constellations. She found Pegasus and Aquarius. Those aren't easy ones, either."

"Thanks, but you helped me find Andromeda." Kelsey's eyes sparkled and the girls exchanged smiles for what felt like the first time in ages.

Ashlynn had worked some kind of minor miracle. And even though Nina feared a crisis brewing at home, she still took a moment to appreciate the joy of seeing a warm, sisterly bond between her girls.

Hoping to keep the happy mood inside the cabin for at least a little longer, Nina kept the conversation going to prevent the girls from seeing their dad's body language outside. "How was ziplining?"

Ashlynn fluffed her dark curls, the sound of her thin metal bracelets sliding and clanging. "Well, that part of our day got canceled because of another kind of excitement."

"Really?" Nina asked in surprise, grateful for the distraction from her worries. "What happened?"

Kacie swallowed down her cookie before launching to her feet, full of animation. “A rabid dog came running out of the woods, right at us.”

A fresh layer of her already-mounting panic tore through her chest. Images of a foaming, lunging dog had her trembling, reaching to check over her children and be sure they were unharmed.

Ashlynn rested a reassuring hand on Nina’s arm. “The dog wasn’t rabid and no one got charged. And definitely no one was bitten, or even scratched. The dog had a collar with a rabies tag. And it also had a litter of puppies.”

Kacie continued, talking in rapid-fire excitement, “When we called the vet to trace the rabies tag, they found the owner. Some jerk dumped the mama and her babies in the woods. But we called Mr. and Mrs. O’Brien and they came with all the right equipment to catch them safely and take them back to the ranch. It was so exciting, right, Kelsey?”

“Sure was,” Kelsey agreed. “Their vet is looking over them now, but Mrs. O’Brien said if the doctor gives the okay, we can come see the puppies later, as long as we don’t get too close. If you give us permission.”

Kelsey clasped her hands together. “Please, please, please.”

Kacie offered the plate of cookies like a bribe. “Pretty please.”

Taking a sugar cookie with orange sprinkles, Nina glanced at the window. Douglas was still on the phone, pacing. The tension in his shoulders and his jaw indicated the news was bad. Really bad. What if they had to leave early? The girls would be devastated.

And so would she. She hadn’t realized until just this moment how strong the flicker of hope had grown inside her after her night with Douglas, and she had no idea what to do with that.

Her hands trembling, she set her cookie on a napkin before she crushed it. “We’ll see. First, I need to talk with your father.”

To find out if they were one step closer to losing their home. She couldn’t imagine any other scenario that would have Douglas so worked up. A sick animal would be upsetting, but they could manage a vet bill. This looked like something bigger.

As she stared down at the plate of cookies, her vision blurring with tears, she wanted to hope they could still save the farm. She’d told Douglas so often that they could do it if they thought outside the box and looked for more ways to generate income. But had she been delusional? Desperate? Deep down, she couldn’t help but fear that her insistence they could save the place was nothing more than a need to replace what she'd lost as a kid.

Douglas charged up the cabin steps, mentally clicking through what he needed to accomplish before hitting the road to go home. Movement had always been his answer, his default setting when his carefully curated plans exploded.

Today was no different.

Striding through the cabin's great room, he dimly registered the girls offering him cookies. He swiped a couple off the plate, going through the motions of politeness on his way to the bedroom. He stuffed the cookies in his mouth, on autopilot as he clicked on the lights and tugged out his old brown duffel.

All he had to do was get packed. That was the plan of action after his conversation with the Jacksons. Pack now. Drive. Figure out a plan.

The motor on the vacuum pump for their primary milking machine had burned out. And since Hershel Jackson was a seasoned mechanic, if he said it was busted beyond repair, that was as good as a death sentence for the machinery.

There wasn't enough money in the bank to purchase a new one, and without the current one in good working order, he wasn't even sure he could get a decent bid on the property. Certainly not as much as he would need to put a down payment on a place for Nina to live with the girls.

If they couldn't keep up with the cows' milk production, the animals would be in agony, even risking infection. Repairs would be costly, but absolutely crucial.

His hands clenched into fists, his fingers digging into the thick flannel of his folded shirts. With a steady breath—steadiness he did not feel—he tossed his shirts into the suitcase.

Levelheaded, cool action was needed.

But at what cost?

So much for changing the trajectory of his life. He'd enjoyed what—a whole few hours of hope for the farm? He should have known there was no way to buy into Nina's pie-in-the-sky notions that somehow the family land could be saved. He'd known months ago that he'd given it his best and his best wasn't enough. It had been purely wishful thinking to believe anything different.

Anger at the injustice of it all left a sour taste in his mouth that threatened to undo him.

Douglas heard the door click shut. Without looking up, he could feel Nina's eyes boring into his back. The weight of her stare added to the burden of failure already bludgeoning him.

She cleared her throat. "What did the Jacksons have to say?"

He didn't turn around, couldn't face her as the impact of their predicament struck deep into him. He opened another drawer, pulling out socks. "What are the girls doing?"

"They're with Ashlynn. She's taking them to the pumpkin-carving party." She touched his arm. "Douglas? You didn't answer my question. What did the Jacksons have to say when you talked to them?"

"I have to go." His eyes flickered to hers and caught there for a moment.

"The girls are going to be crushed."

The disappointment on her face was so much Douglas had to turn away. He broke their gaze, heading to the tall wardrobe in the corner of the room.

Nina's boots tapped lightly as she moved over to toward him. Stopped short. The space between them was an abyss, a world.

"Douglas, what happened?" The softness of her tone, the caring beneath it, reminded him of how close he'd been to recovering a life together just an hour ago.

He steeled himself against the cavern full of feelings he didn't have time to deal with. Impatient to be on the road, he grabbed a couple of shirts off the hangers.

"I didn't say you and the girls have to come home. Just me." He jammed the clothes into his bag.

Her head snapped back. She dragged in a breath and then repeated, "What happened?"

"The primary milking machine broke." He zipped the bag. Marched to the bathroom for his razor. "It's irreparable. I have to figure out what to do with our herd."

"I'll come with you. Maybe the girls can stay here with Ashlynn. I can help."

"I've got it handled." The thought of her seeing more ways their family home was falling apart made him sick to his stomach. "I'll figure out how to salvage things somehow."

She sagged to sit on the edge of the bed. "If you're already determined to give up and sell the place, what does it matter how bad the problem is?"

He bristled at the argumentative tone in her voice. "Nina, we have responsibilities to the animals in our care until the day comes to sell them."

"And the Jacksons can handle things until the kids and I can pack, too." Flames danced in her amber eyes.

"My farm is not the Jacksons' responsibility."

She fixed him with a stare. Face tight, lips thinning into a tight line. “Your farm? *Your* farm? Like the girls and I are just guests and it’s not our home, too?”

“That’s not what I meant.”

“But it’s what you said. Douglas, you’re shutting me out again, and that hurts, even worse than before because you gave me hope that you could change.” She stood in front of the door, searching his face. “You’re choosing to push me away. Is that what you truly want?”

Even with everything riding on his answer, he couldn’t come up with the words she needed. “Real life isn’t like a communication class at the Top Dog Dude Ranch.”

Even as he said it, he could feel the air leave the room. Without a word, Nina stepped aside, clearing the way for him to leave.

He steeled his resolve, using it to insulate himself against this final blow, the worst loss of all. The loss of his family. Because there was no doubt, he’d just lit a match to the wreckage of his life.

Chapter Thirteen

Nina was destroyed. Shattered. She wanted to curl up in bed and cry herself to sleep for days. But the girls wanted to pick second-season crops with their new friends. Ironic since they had to be hog-tied to do those same chores at home.

Home.

Her throat closed.

The pain of Douglas's about-face was all the more painful because of the stupid, stupid way she'd allowed herself to hope he'd changed. Yet at the first sign of trouble, he'd gone right back to being the Douglas of before.

Distant. Shutting her out.

Sitting cross-legged on a quilt beside her sister, Nina cradled a mug of hot apple cider in one hand and stroked the purring calico cat in her lap with the other. Eyes tracking her daughters as they pulled carrots out of the ground, she inhaled warming scents of cinnamon and the tang of still-damp dirt. She'd offered to join them, but their horrified expressions made it clear she would cramp their style with their new buddies.

At least that gave her more time to enjoy the last bit of Ashlynn's visit. She needed her sister, needed to pour out her heart to someone who knew her well and wouldn't judge.

Because she'd messed up her life and she didn't know how to make things right. Douglas had driven off right after their fight, the truck kicking up a cloud of dust on his way back to their farm. She hadn't heard a word from him. He wasn't answering calls or texts. She fluctuated from mad to worried to angry all over again. He'd spent their entire trip at the ranch trying to woo her, only to cut her off when they should be closer than ever.

And just that fast, her anger shifted to hurt.

Blinking back tears, she stared down into her cider, steam winding through the air before fading.

Ashlynn nudged her knee, cupping her own mug of cider. "The girls seem to be enjoying themselves."

Nina attempted a smile, trying to locate the same source of optimism Ashlynn continuously drew from. Her sister made hope look as effortless as her elegant dark curls. "I'm glad Jacob and Hollie let them see the puppies after the veterinarian cleared them and was checking over the protective mama dog."

"Weren't those the cutest puppies ever?" Ashlynn stirred a cinnamon stick in the paper mug. "You would hardly recognize them from when we saw them in the woods."

There were nine puppies, approximately three weeks old, fluffy and alert. Some were yellow, some chocolate. The girls hadn't been allowed to touch them, but they'd stared entranced for a solid twenty minutes.

Stroking her fingers through the calico's plush fur, Nina continued, "Kelsey's already begging to come back and get one of the chocolate-colored pups when they're old enough. I haven't figured out how to tell her I'm not even sure she'll be able to keep the pets she already has when we move."

"Uhm, it may be nothing, but..." Ashlynn picked at her leggings, a nervous habit from as long as Nina had known her. "Before the girls come back, there's something we need to discuss. I had a conversation with Kelsey while you were gone, and I'm a little concerned."

Nina went cold inside. “How so?”

“She seems really stressed, to the point she kept gripping her stomach and rubbing her forehead. She talked about how upset she’s been with the struggles you and Douglas have had. She even mentioned being scared of moving. She had questions about those feelings being so bad a person could worry about dying.”

“Dying?” Nina pressed a hand to her chest over her racing heart. That her daughter might have carried such fears had her own stomach roiling. “What did you say to her?”

“I shared some stories about how I felt in foster care, trying to help her label her feelings. I even talked her through a sensory exercise for calming down.” Her cheeks puffed on a hefty exhale.

“Did it seem to help?”

“Tough to tell. Maybe she’s truly sick, but also I know what it’s like for the body to shout when your heart’s hurting. And you have to admit the girls are dealing with a lot of the same problems you are. They’re just viewing them from an even more confusing perspective.” Ashlynn gave her a pointed look. “Do you want to talk about why Douglas tore off like a bat out of hell?”

Truth be told, the roller coaster of emotions had left her at a loss for words. From her lap, the calico had no such trouble articulating her sentiments, mewing softly before stretching an orange-and-black paw to Nina's hand that grasped the cider. Nina scratched the cat's head, taking a beat to gather her thoughts when her heart was breaking in the middle of a world that seemed full of joy.

In front of the quilt edges, a toddler boy with bright auburn hair careened toward his mother. He held a cabbage that was easily half the size of his body. He dropped the vegetable in a slightly worn wooden basket, clapping his hands together in triumph.

Nina tried to tamp down the jealousy brewing in her gut as she looked on at families and young couples gathering carrots and pumpkins. Why was happily-ever-after so easy for everyone else? Leashing the pain, she readied herself to explain the painful turn of events with Douglas to her sister.

"Our night away was going so well. Then the bottom fell out with yet another crisis at the farm and he ran." The memory of his stony expression in the bed they shared floated before her mind's eye. "I need a man who will be there for me. I can't keep wondering when he will check out again."

Ashlynn set her cider down on the quilt and gave Nina's hand a tight squeeze. "Oh, hon, I'm so sorry to hear that."

Tears begged for release, gathering in the corners of her eyes. Blinking up at her, the calico's deep rumbling purr intensified.

"And it's not just me he's hurting. The kids are losing so much." Nina stared off into the distance; about fifty yards away, Kacie and Kelsey were filling a bushel with an assortment of beets, carrots and winter squash. "They complain sometimes about all the work around the farm, but I know they're going to miss the life when we move."

"So you're just giving up on that dream?"

Exasperation had her hands shaking so hard she had to set her cider aside to keep it from sloshing over the side. "He's the one who wants to sell the place. Not me." Remembering those arguments made her mad all over again. "If it were up to me, I would have fought to the bitter end to save my childhood home—if I'd had one."

"And you're absolutely sure there's no hope just because the date night ended on a bad note?"

Settling further into her lap, the calico mewed again until Nina resumed petting. The kitty revved those purrs right back up, vibrating against her hand, keeping her from losing her cool altogether. "Things were better since we came here, and that's what makes his turnaround so hurtful. Although I guess I always knew it would fall apart once we left here."

"Are you saying you believe this place is really full of magic and once you leave, the fantasy fades?"

"Of course I don't believe there's anything mystical about the Top Dog Dude Ranch." The calico's head butted her hand to keep her attention. "The O'Briens just do such a good job at getting people in touch with their emotions, helping them connect."

"And they're the only people who've ever successfully imparted effective couples' counseling?" Ashlynn asked, staring at her over her mug with an arched brow.

"Now you're just being argumentative."

Ashlynn leaned forward, setting her now-empty mug down on the quilt, fixing a gaze full of intensity and caring onto Nina. "Only doing what's needed to walk you to my point. You and Douglas both don't have a great track record at asking for help. Counseling may not repair your marriage, but since things are already falling apart, what can it hurt? And it really could also be a help to Kelsey."

That was the one argument she couldn't refute. "I promise I'll think it over."

"That's all I'm asking." Ashlynn's arms opened wide.

Nina eased the cat from her lap and the calico padded away, tail flicking back and forth. She sank into the hug from her sister—their precious bond a tether in every tempest.

Pulling back from the embrace, Nina dipped her chin toward Kelsey and Kacie, struggling under the weight of their basket. "Let's go help the girls with their haul."

Douglas threw a wrench back into his toolbox, up to his elbows in grease and up to his neck in trouble. His orange tabby launched from behind a stall. Hissing, Waffles leaped onto a half wall, then up to a shelf.

The cold night air iced the sweat on Douglas's brow. He'd worked all day, tinkering with the tubes and wiring on the broken machinery. The sun slunk from view hours ago. He'd lost track as he worked. Dark night sky devoid of stars and heavy with clouds filtered in through the barn's open doors as he surrendered to the inevitable. Hershel Jackson had been right about it being broken beyond repair.

It hadn't taken Douglas too long to get home. Then again, he'd hardly stuck to the speed limit; making calls the whole drive, he'd arranged for neighboring farms to pick up his cows, divvying them up according to how many each spread could handle. It stuck in his craw having to ask for so much help. It was easier giving assistance than accepting it.

Waffles watched with disdainful eyes, tail keeping time like a metronome.

He scrubbed his face, defeat sinking in. Squatting down, he leaned against the barn wall, his muscles sore from hours of bending over the machinery. And for what? Douglas began to wonder if he'd made it worse, like so much else in his life. Nina had begged him so often to keep trying, not to give up on the farm. But it wasn't that simple for him.

Nina was such a leap-of-faith person, a skill he'd never possessed. If he sold now, maybe, just maybe they could still get enough cash for him to buy a little house for Nina and the girls. If he held on and plan B failed? Then he would lose everything, including any hopes of a good credit score.

If ever he'd needed his brother's advice…

The pain of that loss was every bit as fresh today as the day of his brother's accident.

Seeing his brother fall, running, full out trying to save him. Even knowing there was no way to make it before his brother hit the ground, still he pumped his feet hard. He tried.

And he failed.

He'd dropped to the ground beside his brother, calling the ambulance, phone on speaker so his hands were free. He sat beside his brother, trying to keep him talking while not allowing him to move even one iota.

The thought of losing his brother then was incomprehensible. It still was.

He knew he needed to reach out to Nina. Time was slipping away. But he didn't know what to say and feared making things worse. If that was even possible. Just as he'd been frozen there sitting beside his brother, afraid to move, afraid for his brother to move. Immobility was both comforting and infuriating.

And just like that, he could hear his brother's wisdom seep through, all the times Tyler had cautioned him about burying his head in the sand to avoid an argument. All the times Tyler had told him to let his feelings out after their parents' deaths.

All the same things Nina accused him of.

He looked around his barn, the space so full of scars from repairs and patches it was a miracle the four walls were still standing. Was there really a chance the place could be saved as Nina claimed? Could this possibly be an outpost of the Top Dog Dude Ranch? Jacob had mentioned looking to purchase land to open another operation, but might he be interested in a partnership?

It would be a huge risk. A leap of faith.

And hope, a voice whispered from somewhere inside his head.

The last two weeks had shown him how addictive that feeling of hope could be. He'd felt it with Nina. Sensed the possibility of a happier future with her if only he could see beyond the failures of the past to make real changes. Choose a different path.

Was he going to do that? Or bury his head in the sand again? He knew what Tyler would have said. Douglas owed it to Nina and his girls to try harder. Dig deeper, right?

For the sake of his family he intended to explore new possibilities for this place. Because Nina had more than his last name.

She had his heart.

Adjusting the filter on her camera, Nina captured images of the Strutt Your Mutt parade, full of people and animals in costume. How surreal that they'd already reached their final weekend at the Top Dog Dude Ranch.

The past few days at the ranch without Douglas had been so empty, so full of hurt. She cried herself to sleep, face buried in her pillow so the girls wouldn't hear her. And for the girls, she was making her best effort to get through this day even though the happiness all around her stung like alcohol on paper cuts. One photo at a time, she used her art as a shield from the hurt, rather than as a joy.

She zoomed in on a pirate escorting his beagle dressed like a parrot. Losing herself in her art offered a welcome distraction from worrying about the end of their time at the ranch. Would that mark the start of her life as a single mom? She'd been so sure just two weeks ago. And now?

She wanted something she couldn't have. A whole and connected family.

At least they would have the Harvest Festival to distract them on their last weekend. Nina was grateful for the extra celebration for the girls, even as she struggled to make it through the day. Apparently this was a tradition at the ranch. Hollie and Jacob had been opening up their grounds to the public this time of year ever since they began their business for a Halloween parade and Barktoberfest games spread out in a cleared field. A giant tic-tac-toe board made of planks was set up off to one side. Children dressed like mermaids and pirates gathered around a rustic wooden table with small pumpkins. The corn toss drew a group of four teenagers from town in a zombie-versus-vampire competition.

Halloween—the frenzied candy rush and silly costumes—was apparently Hollie's favorite holiday. She had told Nina she liked to see folks come together to laugh.

Her girls certainly took the idea of laughter to heart. While they both opted to dress up as clowns, they'd taken the concept in vastly different directions.

Kacie, outfitted as a rodeo clown, played one of the games, scrunching her face as she tossed ears of corn into a bucket. Her painted cartoonish mouth curved with elation when the corn clanged into the bucket, success lighting her features as she high-fived her sister.

Nina snapped photos in rapid succession, capturing the sweet moment between the girls. She wanted to hold on to every incarnation of joy as tightly as possible, to use the photographs as armor in the years to come.

Remembering her promise to share pictures with Hollie, Nina peeled her camera from the giggling twins. Vendor stations stretched in a line, filling the air with mouthwatering scents of caramel apples, roasted peanuts, hot corn dogs. Popping corn pinged inside a large metal pot, savory butter melting in a pan off to the side.

While *magic* wasn't the right word for the atmosphere, *enchantment* was. She took refuge in the artistic impulses stirring to life in spite of the hole in her heart. She imagined a print or two from the festival hanging in Hollie's ice cream shop. The fleeting daydream felt like a testament to the power of this place.

Dreaming felt dangerous. Especially now. But hope—ridiculous as it seemed—kept calling to her. A siren song that belonged to art, the power of creation, the surge of possibilities.

She lowered her camera, taking in the parade. Townsfolk and Top Dog Dude Ranch participants alike walked down the route. A new arrival dressed as a beekeeper walked a little bumblebee bulldog puppy. Little Red Riding Hood and the Big Bad Wolf marched with their leashed pugs dressed like three little pigs.

The grandmother, daughter and granddaughter trio wore fairy wings, accompanied by a Labrador retriever wearing a gnome hat.

Bopping her head to the twang of the nearby banjo, Kelsey tugged on the hem of her skirt. As a Harlequin clown, Kelsey had opted for a more glam—and classic—costume than her sister. "Too bad Dad couldn't get back for the color run this morning."

Nina adjusted the zoom on her camera, focusing on the Smooch Your Pooch kissing booth raising funds for a local animal shelter. A rough collie with a lion's mane costume was the current pooch folks could take a picture with. "Aunt Ashlynn did a good job standing in before she left. We placed third."

Kacie stuffed cotton candy into her mouth. "We could have been first if Dad had been here."

"Is Dad going to make it back in time for the party tonight? I want him to see my costume." Kelsey twirled on one foot like a ballerina, then almost lost her balance. Her arms reached for Kacie, whose steady presence kept her from falling. A dachshund dressed as a crayon barked from the parade route.

"I'm not sure, sweetie." Nina lowered her camera to look her daughter in the eyes, her heart squeezing. "He texted that he's on his way as soon as he wraps up things at the farm."

He'd finally called her, but had kept the conversation brief—so painfully brief. He'd just told her the basics on what he'd done to secure their animals and said they needed to talk in person. She'd thought at one point she detected a hint of something upbeat in his voice, pushing past his exhaustion. But she'd been mistaken so many times over the years she just couldn't bring herself to repeat past mistakes by grasping at false hope.

"Girls, let's enjoy today and if he doesn't make it in time, you can tell him all about it on the ride home."

Kelsey rubbed her temple. "I wish Aunt Ashlynn could have stayed to see all of this. She said being here reminded her of the time she lived with us. I miss her."

"So do I, kiddo, so do I." Nina let the camera hang around her neck. Pulling Kelsey toward her, she slid her arm around her daughter and squeezed her tight.

Ashlynn had a way of cutting right to the heart of the matter. It was one of the things she admired about her sister.

And Ashlynn had managed to pick up on Kelsey's anxiety in less than a day when Douglas and Nina missed it living in the same house.

How strange she'd never realized Kelsey was a lot like Douglas. Both of them held all their worries inside.

Alone in bed the night before, Nina had read a lot about the physical manifestations of anxiety, certain Ashlynn had a point. Nina had asked Kelsey to share about the sensory calming exercise Ashlynn taught her, and Kelsey's earnest determination to get it right broke Nina's heart.

And truth be told, right now Nina's insides were every bit as torn up by fears as Kelsey's had been. She felt like that young teen again, orphaned, with no idea what her future held. Aching to have her family back, but knowing there was no way to recreate what once was.

And feeling completely ill-equipped to put all the pieces together to bring a vision for something new into focus.

A squeal cut her thoughts short. Kacie jumped up and down, waving, her rodeo clown hat flopping. “Whoo hoo! Dad’s back.”

Chapter Fourteen

Douglas could still feel the strength and love in his daughters' hugs. Their squeals of welcome echoed in his ears even as they gathered for supper. The evening's chili and pie cook-off was situated alongside the corn maze, moonlight and tiki torches cutting the darkness in the field between the main ranch house and the barn. The costume parade had ended, with most of the locals heading for home after dinner, but here and there a winged fairy or masked pirate would streak past with a parent.

Now evening activities were beginning for the ranch guests, the air buzzing with the low hum of laugher and after-dinner conversation highlighting another Top Dog success. The ranch had shown Douglas how good life could be if he took stock of all that he already had.

As if he didn't have enough driving him to fight for his family—for his wife. He'd been trying to find the right time to get her alone since he returned, even if he didn't have a plan yet.

And finally, his daughters were parked in a nearby clearing with a dozen other kids for a sing-along, complete with babysitters to keep watch and feed them dinner.

Nerves kicked up his pulse. He turned to his wife, and they both spoke at once.

He said, "We have to talk—"

"There's something I have to tell you," she announced, then stopped short. "You first."

Curiosity, hope and dread mixed into a strange intoxicating tonic. "No, you go ahead."

She glanced over at the kids, both engrossed in a rousing chorus of "Home on the Range."

"Follow me." Nina gestured toward the corn maze. "We need to go somewhere we can both hear clearly."

He would have thought she was propositioning him, except she tugged at her camera strap in the way she did when she was stressed.

"You look worried." He touched the small of

her back lightly, the simple contact sending a jolt of awareness through him. Was she unhappy with him—rightly so—after the way he'd left? "What's wrong?"

She walked deeper in the maze, the moonlight shimmering off her golden-blond hair. "I had a conversation with Ashlynn before she left that really has me worried."

Alarms sounded in his head. What else could go wrong? He hated always being on the lookout for the next crisis. "About what?"

Nina stopped, pivoting to face him, her dark eyes so troubled it broke his heart. He wanted to stroke back her hair, gather her into his arms, but her arms were tight across her chest defensively.

"Ashlynn's concerned that the stress of our marital problems is taking a toll on Kelsey to the point she's developing some physical symptoms."

The echo of banjo music faded as his world narrowed. He jammed his hands into his pockets. "What do you mean by physical symptoms?"

"Stomach pains, headaches, things like that." Her shoulders sagged, but her arms stayed folded across her chest. "Ashlynn said they seemed to be tied into anxiety about all that's been going on with Tyler, with money problems…and with us." Her fingers gravitated to the camera strap again.

"I think we need to talk to Kelsey about this before we leave."

To tell their daughter what? He was at a loss, so far out of his emotional depth he questioned how in the world he would be able to win back his wife. "What do you think we should say to her?"

"Well, we can't say everything will be all right when there's no way we can guarantee that." She looked up at him, shrugging, her beautiful brown eyes so sad it tore his heart in two. "We do the only thing we possibly can do. We need to be honest."

"Or maybe we can just ask her what's wrong, see what she says, and take it from there." Where had that come from? He'd always deferred to Nina when it came to parenting.

But it just seemed to him that they'd all done a lot of assuming what the other was thinking or feeling without asking. Four separate entities moving through life, rather than a cohesive family.

Nina eyed him with confusion, and more than a little surprise. "Sure, that's actually a smart way to handle it."

"It's been my experience lately that no matter how hard I plan, life throws curveballs at me, left and right. I can see how Kelsey might feel the same and be struggling to put those feelings into words."

"Ashlynn suggested counseling." She eyed him

warily. "Is this something you would consider? For us, too?"

He drew in a shaky breath, taking hope in the fact that she was even willing to consider counseling, when just two weeks ago she'd been ready to call it quits. "I know I've screwed up and I want to fix it. I just need you to be patient a little while longer so I can do this in my own time."

"Douglas, our time here at the ranch is running out and I can't keep holding on forever."

There was a vulnerability in her eyes that told him he could kiss her, here alone in the corn maze away from prying eyes, that he could press the advantage, kiss her and kiss away all the pain he'd caused her.

But he could see she wasn't ready to forgive him for walking away, and they also needed to put Kelsey's mind to rest about whatever was in her heart. And while he'd learned about listening, he'd also discovered the wisdom of waiting for the right time. Not avoiding, just preparing.

His wife, the love of his life, deserved to be swept off her feet with romance and the reassurance he was a man she could trust with forever.

The next afternoon, Kelsey stood on the split-rail fence around the corral, watching her sister compete in the Top Dog junior rodeo. She was really proud of her, and that was a lot easier to admit now that her sister wasn't saying mean things to her all the time. How crazy to think that they would be going home tomorrow.

Every junior rodeo competitor had been paired with a ranch hand for the team roping event. Kacie had spent the morning nervously fidgeting with the brim of her pale blue cowboy hat that matched her button-up shirt. But once her twin sat on the horse? All the nerves were swapped for a serenity Kelsey didn't quite understand but envied.

A clang and squeak announced the opening of the gates. Kacie and Apple moved forward at a quick, controlled lope toward the quick-moving calf.

Cheering, Kelsey leaned forward, almost toppling. Her mom and her dad each clasped one of her shoulders.

"Careful, kiddo," her dad said. "It's exciting, isn't it? Your sister's really kicking butt out there."

Right arm circling wide, Kacie aligned herself with the calf. Her rope and the ranch hand's rope landed spot-on. Perfect form and the quickest time yet.

She advanced to the lead. Exciting. And not surprising. Kelsey cheered until her throat was raw. Then she looked at her dad.

"Kacie's a lot smarter than she thinks." Kelsey

just wished Kacie knew it. Maybe she would if she won today's junior rodeo match.

Her mom swept back her braid. "That's perceptive of you to say. I hope it's a sign that you two are getting along better."

Having both her parents here beside her, not fighting, life was almost normal. "Yeah, she's being a lot nicer since we got here."

From across the dirt arena, Kacie flashed a smile, beaming at the accomplishment. Kelsey returned the gesture and threw her sister two thumbs up. Nodding, Kacie patted Apple's neck.

The next event—barrel racing—was about to begin.

Her dad hitched a hip against the fence, angling sideways to look at her. "You still seem, uh, stressed. Is there something on your mind?"

Pursing her lips tight to hold in the words, she shook her head. All her excitement over her sister took a back seat to a burning sensation in her stomach. She stepped down from the fence. "No, nothing, I'm going to go find my book."

"Hold on." Her dad touched her arm lightly. "Are you sure there's nothing we should know?"

She kicked a worn tennis shoe through the dirt. "I just don't feel good today. That's all."

Her mom knelt in front of her. "What's hurting? Maybe there's something we can do if we know."

This was such a great day for her sister, and her parents seemed to be getting along. She hated to ruin that. She glanced back to Kacie, who waited in a line of four horses and riders. Top Dog staff set the bright blue barrels out into the arena, making sure they were appropriately spaced for the competitors.

Jacob read the first name over the loudspeaker. An eleven-year-old boy coaxed a black gelding forward into a gallop.

Kelsey let out a deep breath. She'd tried so hard to keep her problems to herself so her parents could fix theirs, but now everything was coming out at the worst time, right when they should be focusing on Kacie. "It's just my stomach and my head. There's nothing anybody can do."

Her gaze flashed to Kacie, but it wasn't her turn yet.

"Kelsey, kiddo," her mom said, taking Kelsey's hands in hers and leading her to a wooden bench. "Your dad and I love you very much, and we are so very proud of you. You know that, right?"

Her legs folded, and she sank to the bench. "I love you guys, too, and I try really hard not to disappoint you."

Her mom smoothed a hand over her head. "Sometimes when we put a lot of pressure on ourselves or when life is rough, our bodies show symptoms of the stress. My stomach used to hurt so badly right before a test, or when I went to a new foster home."

Her dad sat on her other side. "Or how my head pounds when something breaks on the farm."

All the fear and worries piled up inside her until it bubbled over. She couldn't keep the words inside any longer. "Is that why Uncle Tyler had that aneurysm? Because he was worried about losing the home where he grew up? That he worried until he died?"

"Kelsey, kiddo, no," her dad insisted so quickly it sounded like he was telling her the truth. "An aneurysm is a medical condition someone is born with. His death had nothing to do with financial problems."

Her mom and dad exchanged one of those long, pointed looks before her mom smoothed a hand over her braid. "Are you worried about your headaches?"

Kelsey blinked fast against the sting of tears. "I don't want to make you guys worry and get sick, too."

Her mother drew her in for a hug. "Kelsey, honey, it's never even dawned on us you would worry about that. But when Tyler first became ill, we asked the doctor if it was genetic. He said it was a result of Tyler's high blood pressure because

Tyler didn't take his medications. If you want us to talk to the doctor together, we can make an appointment. But truly, you're a healthy ten-year-old girl."

Kelsey scrubbed a hand over her blurry eyes. Could it really be that simple? What her mom said made sense, and her dad wasn't arguing.

Another horse and rider, the last competitor, whizzed past them. The pace was so fast, she almost didn't register that it was Kacie and Apple. Her sister took the first barrel—a blur of blue and red.

Her stomach settled a little, like when she ate crackers, but better. She blinked her burning eyes, watching her twin's every move. Still, she couldn't help but ask, "So the headaches? And stomachaches? They're because I'm upset?"

"That's certainly possible," her dad said, in that deep, calm voice of his that made the world better, a voice he hadn't used in a long time. "This is also something we can talk to the doctor about. Would you like to do that?"

"Yes, please." She nodded fast. "As soon as we get home. Thank you."

Around her, the crowd grew frantic, screaming Kacie's name as her sister and Apple galloped faster and faster. An eruption of clapping and whistles echoed.

Kelsey hugged her mom and her dad, hard, and they both hugged her back at the same time. And for a moment, they were a family again. They were her parents, making sure she was okay.

It would still hurt if they split, but at least she could stop worrying that her parents were going to lose her. She'd been so stressed about that, and now, how quickly that giant fear deflated like an old birthday balloon.

Looking at the time on the board, she saw that Kacie beat all previous times by two seconds. And everyone in the junior rodeo had been older than her by two or three years. With the winning barrel race time and the team roping points, Kacie was the clear winner. Kelsey heard her sister let out a victory whoop.

And anything, absolutely anything, felt possible.

Nervously tapping her foot in time with the country band, Nina could hardly believe that this was it, the last event in their two-week retreat. The Fur Ball costume party was in full swing, the barn decked out in lights and lanterns, hay bales and sunflowers.

Nina smoothed her hands down her milkmaid costume she'd chosen in honor of their farm. And yes, she couldn't deny she'd also picked it for the sassy look that she hoped would catch her husband's eye. Long ago, he'd said he enjoyed the light her playful side brought to his life. Somehow worries had ironed that out of her.

So much of her time at Top Dog ranch reacquainted Nina with aspects of herself she'd lost sight of.

She just hoped he got to see it since he'd been running late, just saying he needed to have a quick chat with Jacob O'Brien.

Although Jacob was on stage introducing the band members from Raise the Woof—all employees from the ranch. Now familiar faces from Top Dog held guitars, microphones, drums and a keyboard, including the two stable hands who had been flirting with each other at the bonfire.

She couldn't resist snapping quick photos of the people who'd become like family to her over these past fourteen days. In fact the camera stilled her nerves as she waited for her husband.

So many creative costumes, and so many faces looked lighter than two weeks ago. The firefighter was so relaxed and joyful, she almost didn't recognize him. His wheelchair was decked out, resembling an elaborate throne. Scepter in hand, his eyes full of light, he gazed at his fiancée. Her crown looked like liquid starlight, glittering with faux diamonds, a feminine twin to the firefighter's heavier golden crown adorned with rubies.

Levity and laughter painted the faces of the grandmother, daughter and granddaughter, the trio dressed like the makings of a s'more—graham cracker, chocolate bar and marshmallow.

Nina was happy for them. Truly. She just hoped there was some of that magic left for her family. She kept turning the past two days over in her mind, how she'd been so sure Douglas was going to kiss her in the corn maze, how good he'd been with Kelsey. Something seemed to have changed in him. She could almost forget the way he'd stormed off when the machinery broke and then refused to talk to her.

Almost.

An upbeat electric guitar note hummed in the night air as couples and families made their way to the makeshift dance floor. Toying with her pigtails, she picked her way across the perimeter of the dance floor.

Off to the right of the purple-hued stage, Hollie and Jacob paid homage to their Scottish heritage in a matching red-plaid kilt set. Hollie held her small Scottish terrier pup in her arms, its pink tongue licking her face.

"I don't even know how to thank you for all of this over the past two weeks," Nina said by way of greeting, hands stretched to encompass not only the Fur Ball, but the ranch.

A hand fell to rest on her shoulder. Startled, she looked back and found her husband, looking so big and handsome and adorable in the wholesome milkman's costume she'd picked for him.

"Thanks, Jacob," Douglas called out. "Thanks for everything. I'll get back to you about your offer once my lovely wife and I have a chance to discuss it."

Surprise rooted her feet to the floor. Discussion? She tried to unscramble her thoughts, which would have been difficult to do regardless, and was virtually impossible with the music, dancing and chatter of the gala all around them.

Then Douglas slipped a strong arm around her waist and guided her out of the barn. God, it was scary feeling this hopeful. Although hadn't he said something similar to her? Something about being afraid something else bad would happen?

How had they both become so distrustful of everything?

Douglas stopped outside the corn maze, swept off the white cap and tucked it in his back pocket. He scrubbed a hand over his strong jaw, his gaze sliding back up to meet hers and hold with an intensity in his electric blue eyes that broadcast just how important this moment was to him. "So, about my conversation with Jacob, if you're still on board, I'd like us to try to save the farm."

Shock rippled through her. She wavered a little on her feet, one arm brushing the rough edge of a hay bale stacked near the entrance to the maze. "Really? You want to try to hang on to the farm, even though it's more of a risk now with the latest machinery break? You're serious?"

"I'm skeptical that it can work, but I'm willing to consider options." He cupped her arms. "Together. Jacob is looking to expand, and we have land with the perfect setup for Top Dog II."

Hearing the excitement in his voice, seeing his eyes alive with hope, she couldn't stop from swaying toward him. She just barely stopped herself from leaning the rest of the way in and kissing him, which would end what promised to be the most important conversation of her life. "Jacob and Hollie have been talking about their long waiting list."

"Exactly. Jacob wants to discuss the possibility of using that list as a start-up to get the new site up and running," he said confidently. "It would be a massive undertaking and we wouldn't be the sole owners of our farm anymore—"

"But we wouldn't have to move," she whispered the miracle that she'd barely dared hope for. Her husband was offering the dream she'd prayed for since losing her parents.

"We would probably work even harder than before at a time we should be spending more time on our relationship. And that's where Ashlynn—I hope—would come in."

The surprises kept coming. He had her complete attention. "How so?"

"If you agree, I would like to ask her to move back and work for us. I want you to have family close."

She brought a trembling hand to her mouth, overwhelmed in absolutely the best way. "You're ready to welcome magic into our lives."

"Yes, I am. If you're by my side." He took her hands in his. From the barn, a whisper of a slower song with warbling vocals drifted out over them. "I love you, Nina. I've never stopped. I'm sorry it's taken me so long to let you know how important you are to me."

"How important the girls are, you mean?" Her heart thundered, her ears ringing with the weight of years and her long-lasting desire for his touch, his voice. For him.

"How important *you* are. You are my life." He cradled her face in his hands. "I can't promise I'll ever be able to get over my fear of having more children—"

"Douglas, I—"

He pressed a finger to her lips. "Hold on. Please let me finish." His blue eyes focused solely on her. "I can't promise I'll ever be able to get over my fear of having more children, but I won't get a vasectomy."

His compromise took her breath away, so unexpected now that she fully understood how deep his scars ran from the girls' difficult birth. The love in his eyes, in his voice, wooed her and humbled her all at once.

Her artistic mind filled with snapshots of the last few weeks. New angles on old scenes. A relearning of her life. Kelsey researching this place, trying to bring and keep her family together. Enlisting Kacie to work so hard with her. Both girls had been instrumental to making this new chance for their future together. And Kelsey had made this trip happen even when she felt alone, frightened that her sickness might be a burden.

If her little girl could do that and be brave beyond her years? Nina could, too. "And I'm sorry for not *seeing* you."

"I'm not sure I follow."

"It's like I put a camera in front of my face and viewed the world through that lens as an excuse to avoid what was really there. I should have seen your pain. Just because you don't express your grief the way I do doesn't make it less valid. That's my fault."

"I didn't give you much to go on," he said drily, pulling her closer. His familiar aftershave comforted her as the slow country melody continued.

"And I was so intent on what I thought a family should be, I missed seeing how absolutely perfect the one I have already is."

He rested his forehead against hers. "I love you, Nina Archer. With everything that's inside me, I love you. I want to wake up next to you every morning. I want the honor of growing old with you."

Nina's heart overflowed with joy at hearing her husband say the words she'd always dreamed, having him open up to her in ways beyond what she could have imagined.

Drawing back to take him in, every inch of him so dear. "I love you, Douglas Archer, husband of my heart, love of my life."

She drew his face to hers for a kiss to seal her vow. Douglas was her love…he was her home.

Epilogue

Six weeks later

With laser focus, Kacie eyed her target racing around the corral. Her hands twitched with anticipation, everything she wanted just within reach.

There was just one problem. Her perfect sister was eyeing a different target, and Kacie's heart would break if Kelsey won.

Putting her hands together, Kacie pleaded, "Please, Mom and Dad, please, I want the chocolate-colored boy puppy."

Tail wagging, the chocolate puppy nudged her

hand. Kacie's heart surged, already attached to the sweet boy.

Kelsey pressed her hands to her heart. "But I want the yellow boy puppy over there. I'll do double chores for a month."

Kelsey's preferred puppy rolled on the ground onto his back, tongue hanging out to the side. Yips and woofs filled the air as her family clustered together in the fenced area outside the Top Dog Dude Ranch's barn. They'd driven up for the day to visit the puppies and take one back to the farm with them. The litter she and her sister had found in the woods were ready for homes of their own. All the pups had been given a clean bill of health, and the mama dog had already been adopted by the firefighter and his fiancée, the couple who'd been at the ranch with them.

Nine puppies scampered around, so cute and cuddly. The vet said they appeared to be Labrador puppies, with some collie mixed in, making them shaggier. Two golden-colored puppies played tug-of-war with a rope. Four pups chased one another and climbed over a fat tractor tire in a little obstacle course. A couple more snoozed under a wooden bench.

The chocolate boy, the one Kacie wanted with every fiber of her being, sat in front of her with attentive brown eyes that said he was eager to learn. Adventures they could have together danced through her mind. He would be the best buddy to rope and ride together. She just knew it.

Kacie upped the ante. "I'll do all my homework, without complaining, for the rest of the year."

Her parents looked at each other for a long moment in that parent kind of silent talk, in their own bubble, something they had lost for a while, but that had come back now. Thanks to the Top Dog Dude Ranch. Her mom and dad were even having a meeting with Mr. and Mrs. O'Brien today to sign some paperwork that would make their dairy farm Top Dog II. Her mom would get to use her photography skills taking photos of the guests and people who got married there.

She still could hardly believe it was true. Her dad said it was going to be a lot of hard work, but Kacie wasn't afraid of that. She would be doing what she enjoyed most, and would even get to teach little kids how to use a lasso. Aunt Ashlynn was moving to their farm, too. How cool was that?

Kelsey was doing a lot better, too, not so stressed out all the time. The doctor had given Kelsey a lot of advice. Who would have thought they would all be doing goat yoga? But yoga was now a regular part of their lives when Kelsey needed help calming down.

Then it hit her. What if her parents said they

had to get the puppy Kelsey wanted because she was struggling with anxiety?

Of course they would. And she would have to be okay with that, because they were a family. She loved her sister, and never wanted her to doubt that again.

"Okay, Mom and Dad. It's okay if we get the one Kelsey wants." It was hard to smile, but she did it anyway. Kacie knelt to stroke *her* puppy to say goodbye, while her sister squealed and scooped up the yellow fur ball.

Her dad ruffled her hair. "That's really kind of you, Champ. I'm proud of you."

Then her parents exchanged another one of those looks where they talked without words, finishing up their silent "conversation" by nodding.

Her mom knelt beside her. With a really big smile, she tucked one of Kelsey's loose hair strands behind her ear. "How about this? What if you each got a puppy? Do you think you could handle all the work it would take since you wouldn't be sharing the responsibility of just one?"

Kacie looked fast at her sister, and already Kelsey was squealing, "Yes, absolutely yes. We can walk our dogs together. They'll be twins like us."

So excited her chest was about to burst, Kacie stood and locked arms with her sister. "And we know how much work animals are. We won't let you down."

Her dad put his arm around her mom, and she rested her head on his shoulder. Kacie thought for a moment she actually heard their silent conversation, because there was no mistaking that they'd just said they loved each other. They said that a lot lately. There really was something special about the four-legged creatures at the Top Dog Dude Ranch that had given her back her family.

And now, they would be bringing that magic home.

* * * * *

Don't miss the next book in the
Top Dog Dude Ranch miniseries,

The Cowboy's Christmas Retreat

Available November 2021 from
Harlequin Special Edition!

WE HOPE YOU ENJOYED THIS BOOK FROM

HARLEQUIN SPECIAL EDITION

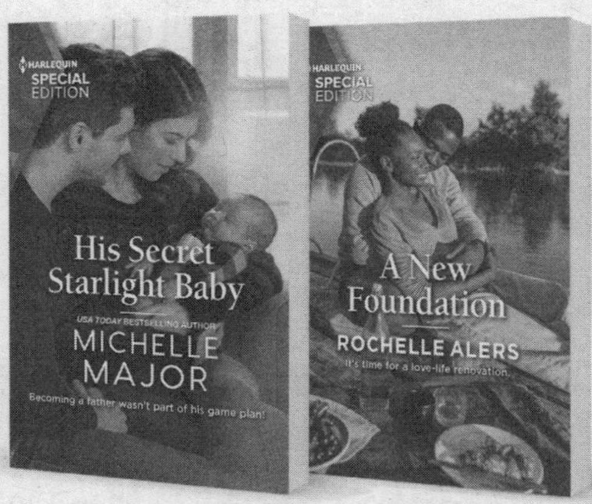

Believe in love. Overcome obstacles. Find happiness.

Relate to finding comfort and strength in the support of loved ones and enjoy the journey no matter what life throws your way.

6 NEW BOOKS AVAILABLE EVERY MONTH!

HSEHALO2021

Uplifting or passionate, heartfelt or thrilling— Harlequin has your happily-ever-after.

With a wide range of romance series that each offer new books every month, you are sure to find the satisfying escape you deserve.

Look for all Harlequin series new releases on the *last Tuesday* of each month in stores and online!

Harlequin.com

HONSALE0521

COMING NEXT MONTH FROM

HARLEQUIN SPECIAL EDITION

#2863 A RANCHER'S TOUCH

Return to the Double C • by Allison Leigh

Rosalind Pastore is starting over: new town, new career, new lease on life. And when she buys a dog grooming business, she gets a new neighbor in gruff rancher Trace Powell. Does giving in to their feelings mean a chance to heal...or will Ros's old life come back to haunt her?

#2864 GRAND-PRIZE COWBOY

Montana Mavericks: The Real Cowboys of Bronco Heights
by Heatherly Bell

Rancher Boone Dalton has felt like an outsider in Bronco Heights ever since his family moved to town. When a prank lands him a makeover with Sofia Sanchez, he's determined to say "Hell no!" Sofia is planning a life beyond Bronco Heights, and she's not looking for a forever cowboy. But what if her heart is telling her Boone might just be The One?

#2865 HER CHRISTMAS FUTURE

The Parent Portal • by Tara Taylor Quinn

Dr. Olivia Wainwright is the accomplished neonatologist she is today because she never wants another parent to feel the loss that she did. Her marriage never recovered, but one night with her ex-husband, Martin, leaves her fighting to save a pregnancy she never thought possible. Can Olivia and Martin heal the past and find family with this unexpected Christmas blessing?

#2866 THE LIGHTS ON KNOCKBRIDGE LANE

Garnet Run • by Roan Parrish

Raising a family was always Adam Mills' dream, although solo parenting and moving back to tiny Garnet Run certainly were not. Adam is doing his best to give his daughter the life she deserves—including accepting help from their new, reclusive neighbor Wes Mobray to fulfill her Christmas wish...

#2867 A CHILD'S CHRISTMAS WISH

Home to Oak Hollow • by Makenna Lee

Eric McKnight's only priority is his disabled daughter's happiness. Her temporary nanny, Jenny Winslet, is eager to help make Lilly's Christmas wishes come true. She'll even teach grinchy Eric how to do the season right! It isn't long before visions of family dance in Eric's head. But when Jenny leaves them for New York City... there's still one Christmas wish he has yet to fulfill.

#2868 RECIPE FOR A HOMECOMING

The Stirling Ranch • by Sabrina York

To heal from her abusive marriage, Veronica James returns to her grandmother's bookshop. But she has to steel her heart against the charms of her first love, rancher Mark Stirling. He's never stopped longing for a second chance with the girl who got away—but when their "friends with benefits" deal reveals emotions that run deep, Mark is determined to convince Veronica that they're the perfect blend.

YOU CAN FIND MORE INFORMATION ON UPCOMING HARLEQUIN TITLES, FREE EXCERPTS AND MORE AT HARLEQUIN.COM.

HSECNM0921

SPECIAL EXCERPT FROM

HARLEQUIN

SPECIAL EDITION

Raising a family was always Adam Mills' dream, although solo parenting and moving back to tiny Garnet Run certainly were not. Adam is doing his best to give his daughter the life she deserves—including accepting help from their new, reclusive neighbor Wes Mobray to fulfill her Christmas wish...

Read on for a sneak peek at The Lights on Knockbridge Lane, *the next book in the Garnet Run series and Roan Parrish's Harlequin Special Edition debut!*

Adam and Wes looked at each other and Adam felt like Wes could see right through him.

"You don't have to," Adam said. "I just... I accidentally promised Gus the biggest Christmas light display in the world and, uh..."

Every time he said it out loud, it sounded more unrealistic than the last.

Wes raised an eyebrow but said nothing. He kept looking at Adam like there was a mystery he was trying to solve.

"Wes!" Gus' voice sounded more distant. "Can I touch this snake?"

"Oh god, I'm sorry," Adam said. Then the words registered, and panic ripped through him. "Wait, snake?"

"She's not poisonous. Don't worry."

HSEEXP0921

That was actually not what Adam's reaction had been in response to, but he made himself nod calmly.

"Good, good."

"Are you coming in, or…?"

"Oh, nah, I'll just wait here," Adam said extremely casually. "Don't mind me. Yep. Fresh air. I'll just… Uh-huh, here's great."

Wes smiled for the first time and it was like nothing Adam had ever seen.

His face lit with tender humor, eyes crinkling at the corners and full lips parting to reveal charmingly crooked teeth. Damn, he was beautiful.

"Wes, Wes!" Gus ran up behind him and skidded to a halt inches before she would've slammed into him. "Can I?"

"You can touch her while I get the ladder," Wes said.

Gus turned to Adam.

"Daddy, do you wanna touch the snake? She's so cool."

Adam's skin crawled.

"Nope, you go ahead."

Don't miss

The Lights on Knockbridge Lane

by Roan Parrish, available October 2021 wherever Harlequin Special Edition books and ebooks are sold.

Harlequin.com

Copyright © 2021 by Roan Parrish

HSEEXP0921

Get 4 FREE REWARDS!

We'll send you 2 FREE Books
plus 2 FREE Mystery Gifts.

Harlequin Special Edition books relate to finding comfort and strength in the support of loved ones and enjoying the journey no matter what life throws your way.

YES! Please send me 2 FREE Harlequin Special Edition novels and my 2 FREE gifts (gifts are worth about $10 retail). After receiving them, if I don't wish to receive any more books, I can return the shipping statement marked "cancel." If I don't cancel, I will receive 6 brand-new novels every month and be billed just $4.99 per book in the U.S. or $5.74 per book in Canada. That's a savings of at least 12% off the cover price! It's quite a bargain! Shipping and handling is just 50¢ per book in the U.S. and $1.25 per book in Canada.* I understand that accepting the 2 free books and gifts places me under no obligation to buy anything. I can always return a shipment and cancel at any time. The free books and gifts are mine to keep no matter what I decide.

235/335 HDN GNMP

Name (please print)

Address | Apt. #

City | State/Province | Zip/Postal Code

Email: Please check this box ☐ if you would like to receive newsletters and promotional emails from Harlequin Enterprises ULC and its affiliates. You can unsubscribe anytime.

Mail to the **Harlequin Reader Service:**
IN U.S.A.: P.O. Box 1341, Buffalo, NY 14240-8531
IN CANADA: P.O. Box 603, Fort Erie, Ontario L2A 5X3

Want to try 2 free books from another series? Call 1-800-873-8635 or visit www.ReaderService.com.

*Terms and prices subject to change without notice. Prices do not include sales taxes, which will be charged (if applicable) based on your state or country of residence. Canadian residents will be charged applicable taxes. Offer not valid in Quebec. This offer is limited to one order per household. Books received may not be as shown. Not valid for current subscribers to Harlequin Special Edition books. All orders subject to approval. Credit or debit balances in a customer's account(s) may be offset by any other outstanding balance owed by or to the customer. Please allow 4 to 6 weeks for delivery. Offer available while quantities last.

Your Privacy—Your information is being collected by Harlequin Enterprises ULC, operating as Harlequin Reader Service. For a complete summary of the information we collect, how we use this information and to whom it is disclosed, please visit our privacy notice located at corporate.harlequin.com/privacy-notice. From time to time we may also exchange your personal information with reputable third parties. If you wish to opt out of this sharing of your personal information, please visit readerservice.com/consumerschoice or call 1-800-873-8635. **Notice to California Residents**—Under California law, you have specific rights to control and access your data. For more information on these rights and how to exercise them, visit corporate.harlequin.com/california-privacy.

HSE21R2

Don't miss the next book in the Wild River series by *USA TODAY* bestselling author

JENNIFER SNOW

In the Alaskan wilderness, love blooms in unlikely places—and between an unlikely couple...

"An exciting contemporary series debut with a wildly unique Alaskan setting." —*Kirkus Reviews* on *An Alaskan Christmas*

Order your copy today!

HQNBooks.com

PHJSBPA1021

Love Harlequin romance?

DISCOVER.

Be the first to find out about promotions, news and exclusive content!

Facebook.com/HarlequinBooks

Twitter.com/HarlequinBooks

Instagram.com/HarlequinBooks

Pinterest.com/HarlequinBooks

YouTube.com/HarlequinBooks

ReaderService.com

EXPLORE.

Sign up for the Harlequin e-newsletter and download a free book from any series at **TryHarlequin.com**

CONNECT.

Join our Harlequin community to share your thoughts and connect with other romance readers! **Facebook.com/groups/HarlequinConnection**

HSOCIAL2021